SOLD TO THE KING

LEGENDS OF BRAEYORK
BOOK ONE

MORGAN RUSH

SOLD TO THE KING

Legends of Braeyork
Book One

by Morgan Rush

Front Cover Art:
DizzyDreamerAI

GET THE FREE SEQUEL!

LOVE LESSONS, (SEQUEL TO SOLD TO THE KING)

Love Lessons is the steamy mini sequel to *Sold to the King*.

It is free for all my subscribers!

And as a subscriber, you'll also learn more about the characters and their juicy secrets, explore maps of the Braeyork Dominion and be the first to know about hot new books in the *Legends of Braeyork* series.

Get your FREE copy at morganrush.com

Follow me and enjoy the *Rush!*

Morgan

Take by the Manbeast

Legends of Braeyork, Book 2

Amazon, Kindle Unlimited, Paperback

Saved by the Warrior Wife

Legends of Braeyork, Book 3

Amazon, Kindle Unlimited, Paperback

Legends of Braeyork, Box Set #1

(Includes first three books and their sequels)

Amazon, Kindle Unlimited, Paperback

ELVA

I had known for years this day would come, but nothing could have prepared me for this. I stood in front of the King and his court, wearing nothing but a thin leather bodice halter and a sheer robe. The gauzy material clung tightly, outlining the generous curves of my tall body.

King Rolfe and his two grown sons stared at me silently. The old grizzled High Meister, standing off to one side, let his mouth gape open. Others in the court, mostly men, feasted hungry eyes upon my backside, murmuring their lecherous approval.

Yesterday I turned nineteen years old.

Today, I was nineteen plus one day—legally a maiden in all the lands of the Braeyork Dominion. I was no longer a girl. Like countless others before me, my father had no choice but to sell me to the King, a sovereign who commanded his subjects with absolute and often ruthless authority. Although greatly feared across the Kingdom, his overflowing treasury also meant he could reward those with whom he found favour.

"What is the name of this virgin?" the King asked, standing up from his red tufted chair a few feet in front of me.

"Elva, your Grace," my father replied. "My firstborn, proclaimed by all who see her as the most desirable virgin in all of Braeyork." He bowed his head. "But of course, you can judge for yourself, Sire."

My father's eyes caught mine momentarily and then quickly turned back to the King. I knew my duty to my three living sisters and the memory of my dead siblings – two cherished brothers and a beloved infant sister. After my mother passed, life in our village grew precarious. We counted ourselves lucky to survive the winter starvations and the waves of pox and black death that swept across Braeyork regularly.

I had been carefully prepared for the King's inspection. My father bartered for the services of a beautician to ensure I would fetch the highest possible price and provide my family hope for a better life. This usual price for a virgin who had just come of age was a few acres of land and a herd of swine or cattle. Or, on rare occasions, a pure Arum gold coin might also be added.

I was not completely downcast about the arrangement if it meant I could prevent more suffering and another dark, hungry winter for my family. I was prepared to leverage the gifts that had been bestowed upon me. As I began to develop a few years ago, it became obvious my face and body were of a rare nature, a pleasing quality that would cause men to stop and stare. My widowed father often told me my future lay within the walls of Braeyork Castle.

I would be sold to the King, and if I used my god-given advantages with skill, I might avoid becoming another concubine to the King and, with luck, become a virgin in waiting, the chance to be his next first-wife. Or perhaps, he might choose me as his second or third wife to provide pleasures unbecoming of a first-wife whose principal role was to bear royal progeny.

Living under the King's mercy meant I would never go hungry again, and my sisters would survive the deathly winters to become maidens themselves.

The beauticians had styled my long white flaxen hair into ringlets—curls that now hung around my face and shoulders, falling down all the way to my thin waist. They shaved me smooth all over, leaving a soft tuft of flaxen hair above the lips of my virgin womanhood they referred to as my 'perfect pussy.'

King Rolfe, aging but tall and powerfully built, stepped closer and touched my chin. "She is as fetching as promised, good sir," he smiled, addressing my father as if I was a broodmare at auction. I knew that was exactly what I was, but I was determined not to show the King any weakness or fear of what fate might await me.

The King waved his two sons forward to join his inspection. "Shane, Aiden. Help me judge her price."

The two sons of the King, who, as everyone in Braeyork knew, were twin brothers, approached and stood beside their father. They were not identical twins. Indeed, they were as different as any two men could be. Shane was fair and handsome, born a few minutes before his brother. He was, of course, the presumptive heir, a heartbeat closer to the throne than Aiden. Shane carried himself with the confidence of a future king.

Every girl I knew swooned over Shane, the Prince of Crasmere. The likeness of his golden locks, smooth face, and blue eyes were painted in countless murals across the Kingdom. Shane touched my shoulder, turning me slightly under his gaze. His spicy, sweet scent pleased my senses.

"Yes, Father. This one is indeed a rare prize," Shane's deep voice echoed across the Hall of Mirrors. He stepped back and eyed me with a smile of the whitest teeth I had ever seen.

The King nodded and moved closer. He put a thick, manicured finger to my lips, gently pried the bottom lip of my mouth open a little, and pushed his finger toward my tongue. I had no choice but to lick his protrusion. The King's eyes held mine, and it was obvious my soft tongue pleased him.

"Aiden, your turn," the King growled as he pushed the finger a little deeper into my mouth, stroking the top of my tongue before slowly withdrawing his royal appendage, leaving me flushed from our brief intimacy.

I stiffened as Aiden, the other brother, approached, and the King moved aside. Aiden stood directly before me, taller and heavier than his brother or father and nearly a head higher than me. His unruly black hair and beard, dark brown eyes, bulging chest, and muscular arms were a stark contrast to Shane's lighter frame and smooth face.

Aiden stared at me with an intensity that caused me to take a step back. I suddenly was unable even to draw breath. He said nothing but inspected me carefully, undressing me as if I stood naked before him. I fought a knot forming in my stomach and a sudden tightness between my legs as I tried to look away from the heat of Aiden's gaze.

"Your name is Elva?" he asked, his voice deep and gravelly.

I struggled to form a reply. "Yes, your…" I wasn't sure how to address him, "your royal highness."

"It's Aiden," he nodded. "And–"

Before he could say anything more, the King interrupted. "Aiden, I see you approve as well." He pointed to the red chair and motioned for his sons to return. Aiden caught my eye, bowed, and followed Shane back toward the King's seat.

"Let me have a closer look," the King announced to the assembled court. He touched my throat lightly with his fingertips, then moved his hands down over my chest. I flinched as his hand covered one of my breasts, squeezing it firmly. It sat heavy in his palm, fingers biting into the delicate flesh. His other hand travelled down my stomach over the sheer robe, touching my flat stomach and coming to rest just above my pubic bone.

I buckled slightly with one hand pumping my breast and the other pushing dangerously close to my shaved pussy lips. His inspection, done in plain view of so many men, including his two sons and the High Meister, not to mention my own father, filled me with a deep sense of embarrassment.

I was about to cry out when he removed his hands, stepped away, and turned to my father. "You spoke the truth in praise of your daughter. I will offer you two hundred acres of fertile land in the Emerald Valley, fifty Ovis Ewes with two Ovis Rams, and twenty coins of pure Aurum gold. Is the price acceptable in exchange for your virgin daughter?"

My father's face lit up. "Indeed, your Grace. Indeed! A most generous offer!"

The King waved to his High Meister. "Zachron, arrange payment to her father, then have the Virgin prepared and sent to my chambers this afternoon."

2

AIDEN

To say I was upset by my father's transaction would not begin to capture my rage as I watched Zachron lead the 'virgin' away. No one had the decency to address her as 'Elva,' the name of the fairest creature I ever had the good fortune to lay my twenty-six-year-old eyes upon.

But to my father, she was just another cunt for his stable. I spat on the cobblestone walkway. I needed to expel even the mere whisper of that vulgar term from my mouth and pray no one would ever refer to her in such a crude manner.

Why does the King, my father no less, need Elva?

He already possesses a harem of fuck dolls and recently married his new young first-wife, Ursula. His second and third wives were carefully chosen for their full-figured, lithe bodies and their willingness to do anything to please the King—day or night.

I watched Elva glide around the corner of the marble staircase leading up to the bathing chamber. The thought of the old High Meister *preparing* this angel turned my stomach. His gnarled, wrinkled hands and long pointy fingernails were not suitable to touch the haunches of a muddy field ox, much less undress and examine the perfection of such a creature as Elva.

I had watched her enter Castle Braeyork with her father. It was not just her stunning beauty that immediately caught my eye; angelic ringlets of snowy white hair encircled her as if she had descended from the clouds like a daughter of the gods.

No, it was more than just physical attraction that drew me to her like a magnet to cast iron.

When I approached her in the Hall of Mirrors, an immediate connection overcame me—a stirring in the very fabric of my gut, the sinews around my heart stretching to try and hold it from bursting. My dry mouth stumbled to form words as I stared at her as if mute and dumb.

I cursed my awkward manner and fear of speaking in public, especially before my father, brother, and the assembled nobility gathered at court this morning. While my brother Shane had a natural gift for such ceremonies, I trembled at the mere thought of public elocution. I prayed I had not made a complete fool of myself before Elva.

And as I drank in her beauty, the roundness of her face, the fullness of her firm haltered breasts, her impossibly narrow waist, and luxuriously long, smooth legs, I fought to control the reaction of my body to the sight of her beauty. My cock, larger even when flaccid than any other man I had ever seen undressing at the bathing pools, swelled within my baggy trousers.

The beast had been duly aroused.

And when Elva replied to my awkward question, with her own flustered response, "your royal highness…" I had to contain the primal urge to sweep her into my arms, lift her sheer robe and taste the dampness of her bare pussy.

I dared dream that only I could pleasure her the way such an angel deserved. And when she was ready, and only after she begged and pleaded and whimpered that her soul belonged to me, and only to me, and would so forever, would I fill the folds of her womanhood with the full length of my hard cock.

And after I spurted deep within her virgin womb, we would lay together in each other's arms—satiated, spent, fulfilled, keeping my cock buried inside her to not allow my cum to seep out.

Instead, I stood in silence, squeezing my legs together to contain my stiff member, gazing at the entrance to the bathhouse a few feet away, where she was being prepared for my father, the King of Braeyork.

3

ELVA

I walked a few steps behind the King's High Meister, Zachron. My mind raced with questions. All eyes were upon me striding from the Hall of Mirrors.

As we turned from the hall into a narrow walkway, I was surprised to see the King's son Aiden, the only man who had shown the decency to speak my name during the negotiations of my sale to the sovereign.

Our eyes caught each other as I brushed by him, dutifully following behind the High Meister. Aiden's bearded face held a strength I had never seen in Saxcoate, the tiny hamlet of my birth and childhood. The intensity of his face, an unexpectedly powerful visage, echoed in my mind as we rounded the corner, and I heard the sound of gently falling water. The sweet fragrance of rose and hibiscus wafted through the moist, steamy air.

"Come child," the High Meister instructed as we approached the sunken bathing pools. Steaming water, fed from one of

Braeyork's many underground hot springs, bubbled over a rock wall into the pool of dreamy milky-blue water. Crimson flower petals floated throughout the pool.

I took a few steps closer to Zachron as he waved at two matronly women who appeared from behind a walled vestibule.

"Bathe her thoroughly," he instructed the women and then, turning to me, commanded coldly, "undress."

His words were spoken with the same tone my father would use to scold a stubborn jackass. I hoped the High Meister would leave me alone with the women for my cleansing bath. But he only stepped aside as one of the women unfastened the leather halter that wrapped around my neck and outlined my large breasts.

The halter also held my sheer robe in place. Once loosened, the robe fell around my feet onto the stone floor. I turned away from Zachron's leering gaze. The women, dressed in modest undergarments, gathered my long white hair into a bun, pinned it atop my head, and guided me down the rock steps. Inside the warm, milky pool, they began to lather my body with a fragrant soap of lavender and shea butter.

They whispered for me to relax. With skilled and delicate hands, they worked efficiently to cleanse me; my breasts, under my arms, my long legs, and then, ever so lightly, the folds of my pussy lips. I squirmed at their touch as the High Meister stared at me from a stool he had dragged to the edge of the pool.

When they finished their ablutions, they helped guide me out of the pool, dabbed me with honeysuckle oil, and unfastened the bun holding my long white hair in place. They arranged some of it to cover my protruding breasts. The rest they let fall behind me and decorated the tail of the ringlets with small blue silk bows that touched the small of my back, just above the cheeks of my ass.

After completing their work, they turned me toward the Meister, still watching from his stool.

"Leave us," he commanded, rising up to approach me. I stood almost naked before him, my snow-white hair covering my bosom, the only thing providing me any vestige of modesty.

I closed my eyes, telling myself to be strong, imagining the joy on my sisters' faces at the news of our family's new-found prosperity. They will feast tonight, I told myself, perhaps dining on the prize sow normally reserved as a hedge against hard times that seemed to show up with dreaded regularity.

The stank odour of the High Meister insulted my nose. It should have been him who the woman scrubbed in the rose-water bathing pool. I forced my eyes open as I felt his hot gaze upon me. He seemed filled with evil intent. I held my breath, dreading what the King had meant by being 'prepared.'

Zachron said nothing to me as he stood within arm's length, close enough that my long arms could grab his wrinkled neck. I had no problem snapping the neck of our cocky barnyard rooster last week, and I was prepared to do the same if the Meister's inspection became too intimate.

I flinched as he touched my face with his bony fingers. His smell, like the stench of a purulent wound, almost made me gag.

His hand moved to my left breast, partially covered by my long hair. He squeezed his fingers around the full girth of it. I gritted my teeth, steeling myself for what I would be forced to do if he dared go much further with his examination. I squeezed my bare legs together, and he stepped back, pulling open the folds of his black robe to reveal his semi-erect, uncircumcised cock.

He touched it and growled. "Show me the gates of your womanhood. I need to ensure for the King that his treasure is intact, as your father so proudly claimed," Zachron hissed.

I froze, unwilling to spread my legs apart for this man.

Stroking his cock with his free hand, the purple head peeking in and out from its wrinkled sheath as he massaged it, he began to slide his hand down over my flat stomach, inching slowly toward my bare pussy. I now might be the property of the King, but I was no obedient fuck doll for the titillation of this perverted High Meister.

I grabbed his hand, wandering down my naked body, and cast it aside with a sure motion. "I belong only to the King," I snorted. "I will not submit to you, or anyone, save King Rolfe himself. Only *he* may examine me in such a personal manner."

My reluctance seemed to excite Zachron. He stroked himself faster, lashing out. "You are nothing, wench! A poor girl without manners. You will submit to my probing, or I will report your treachery to the–"

"Meister! Stop!"

The command startled both of us. King Rolfe strode towards me, a gold pendant swinging from his neck atop his ruffled white blouse. "Zachron, you heard the maiden. You will not touch her. Do you understand?"

The High Meister bowed his head and closed his robe, hiding his shrinking cock. "Your grace, she has been bathed and prepared as you instructed, but I have not been able to inspect or verify if she is—"

"That is not your concern now, Zachron," the King replied. "I will ascertain her purity. And her future in Braeyork."

Inside the King's private bed chambers, I was instructed to lounge naked on white furs thrown over a soft bed stuffed with gosling feathers. The King showered me with gifts: a gold necklace to wear around my waist and gold 'stockings' – thin crisscrossing gold chains that wrapped around my long shaved legs and tied around my ankles. He also presented me with a choker centred by a sparkling blue stone.

I thanked him as I dressed, adorned only in strands of gold around my legs, waist, and neck.

He poured wine into a pewter goblet and offered it to me.

"I wish to apologize for the High Meister," the King said, sitting on a stuffed chair at the foot of the bed. "Drink up, Elva. It may warm you and purge memories of your encounter. I want you to feel safe, always, with me."

"Yes, my grace," I replied, sitting up and tasting the dark, ruby-colored wine. The first sip bit my tongue with its sharp flavor, but I raised the glass and swallowed a mouthful seeking the promised relief. The image of Zachron stroking his organ still lingered.

"Few maidens would dare disobey the High Meister," King Rolfe chuckled. "But I see your spirit is… somewhat untamed, unusually strong, for one so innocent."

I smiled and drank a little more wine, enjoying the pleasant warmth that followed. "I am the oldest in my family and have had to fight hard to protect my…" I hesitated. My virginity was prized not only by my father and King Rolfe but also by me. "To protect my purity, a gift to be opened only by the man to which I will give my heart— my husband."

"Ah… while you may act like a fearless woman beyond your years, you remain as naive as a schoolgirl. You are innocent in the ways of men. That is why you must trust me completely." He smiled. "So I may protect you."

He stood up, adjusting his trousers as he studied me, lounging naked before him, my legs and waist wrapped in golden strands. "The High Meister is a rude man, but he was trying to ensure the petals of your flower have never been opened to anyone."

His voice grew husky. "Show your King the treasure that lies between your legs."

"Yes, your Grace." I moved forward on the fur-covered bed and opened my legs wide for his inspection.

Although I was naked, sitting prone and exposing myself to the most powerful man in Braeyork, I felt no shame. Not only was he the King, but he was also an exceptionally handsome man for his years. He had the fair skin and hair of his son Shane, as well as the dark intensity of his younger son Aiden. I wasn't sure why, but I believed no harm would come to me in the King's presence.

He took a seat on the edge of the bed and touched the calf of my left leg. He stared at my exposed pussy, now within easy reach of his hand. It was bare except for the mound of soft white hair above it.

"You are the most desirable virgin that has ever graced my chamber and laid upon this bed," he whispered, stroking my leg.

His hands, strong and smooth, rubbed lightly over the gold chains and slowly inched toward the folds of my pussy lips. I felt a rush of warmth between my legs as he massaged my inner thigh up and down, each time getting ever closer to the gates of my aroused womanhood.

The King stood up, his eyes fixed upon mine, holding me captive like I was bound to serve him. Still staring directly at me, he cupped his hand over my pussy. He held it a moment, then removed it and wet his index finger in his mouth.

"Have you ever pleasured yourself?" he asked, touching his wet finger to the tiny bud near the top of my pussy. I arched my back at the feel of his touch. I was ashamed to answer his question.

"Have you, Elva?"

I bucked my thighs upward at the sound of my name being spoken by the King. "I… I…"

Could I tell him, yes, I had lately discovered that I could bring pleasure by touching myself? Would he think me a painted fuck doll?

"I…I…"

His finger slowly stroked the hood above my bud, encircling, then coming around and under and over. "Tell me, Elva. There is no need to be ashamed."

"Yes," I cried out, opening my eyes wide. "I have, but never like this." My pussy ached with need.

The King leaned in closer to me as he continued to touch me. "This tiny bud is a maiden's cock," he whispered. "It's called a 'clit.' Say it, and let me know you understand. Tell me what you need to make you cum."

"Touch me!" I cried. "Don't stop!" Waves of excitement trembled through my body.

"Say it, Elva!"

"Rub my clit, your Grace!" I screamed.

"Ohhhhhh…." I was moaning and writhing as he rubbed my clit. Another finger spread my lips, his finger drawing small circles against my wet pussy, his thick finger never moving inside but hitting every sensitive nerve. "Don't stop, please!"

I opened my eyes again, and the sight of his face was enough to put me over the edge. I screamed out in waves of pleasure as I began to lose control. My thighs bucked in the air. I quivered and shook with a deep, warm pleasure.

It took a minute for me to catch my breath. I could feel the wetness of my virgin pussy throbbing with anticipation for the King's cock.

But that was not his plan, even as he removed his garment, revealing the brutish glory of his aging but still muscular frame, including an ample stiff cock between his legs. "I have a new beautiful first-wife, Ursula. Her belly swells with my seed," he said. "And you are much too precious ever to be anything but a first-wife."

He looked at me strangely. "I trust you, Elva. Tell me the truth, and do not lie to me. Are you a virgin?"

"Of course!" I cried. "Do you doubt me? Do you have any way of..." I had no knowledge of how such a thing could be proven, "of checking or..."

He took my hand and pulled me up from the fur-covered bed.

"I don't believe you would lie to me about so precious," he said, speaking plainly, "because if you did, and your husband is disappointed on his wedding night, well, I'm not sure if you would enjoy serving our guests and me as a fuck doll."

"No!" I cried, "please! Believe me, Sire. I have saved myself for marriage."

He smiled. "I believe that you are and will be a virgin for your husband. He will open you for the first time."

I nodded, my face still flushed from the exquisite delighte he had given me.

"But there are other ways you can serve your King, Elva," he added, "without sacrificing your purity."

"I would like to serve you, your Grace. In any manner that pleases you."

"Good," the King smiled and then commanded me sternly, "Rise from the bed and kneel before me."

I slid off the bed and knelt before the naked King. No one had ever touched me in my intimate place before. No one had ever spoken so directly or brought me such indescribable pleasure. I longed to make him as happy as he had made me.

He placed his hands behind my head and pulled me closer, inches from his hard cock. The mushroom-shaped head glistened with drops of his cum. Unlike the High Meister, this one had no foreskin.

"Have you ever seen a circumcised cock?" he asked, gently pushing my face closer to his throbbing manhood.

"Never, your grace." I stared at it, only inches from my face.

"And I'm sure you have never touched one either."

I glanced up at him and shook my head. "I have not your Grace."

He moaned. "Go ahead then, please."

I lowered my eyes and gently touched the tip of his cock, smearing the drops of leaking cum around the head and then feeling the under shaft with my fingers. His stiff cock twitched. I was exciting him and, in doing so, exciting myself.

It felt warm, almost hot, against my fingers. A thick vein pulsed, running along the side and underside. I trailed it with my fingers then gripped and slowly slid my hand over his cock. He moaned as I stroked him.

"Kiss it," he whispered.

The request shocked me but also secretly thrilled me. I stuck my tongue out and gingerly licked the head of his royal cock, swirling around the tip and the droplet of cum hanging from it. I felt him push my head forward like he wanted to feed his cock to me.

He moaned. "Yes, that's it… take it all, Elva."

I opened my mouth a little wider and took the entire head of the King's pulsing cock into my mouth. He held my head and thrust until my mouth was completely filled. His fingers tightened, grabbing strands of my hair, guiding me forward.

"Oh yes… don't stop, Elva," King Rolfe groaned. "I can't take your virgin cunt, but I will fuck your sweet lips."

Holding my head in place, he began to draw his cock from my mouth, thrusting his hips forward to push back in again. Each time I took it from tip to base, my tongue grazing the length of his swollen cock with each thrust.

And then, with another push deep down into my throat, I felt his cock trembling inside my mouth. "Oh yes, Elva. Yes, yes, yes!"

Holding my head firmly, he forced his cock even deeper down my throat. It felt as if it pressed against the back of my tongue. He began to shake. I panicked and tried to pull back, but his strong hold kept his member buried in my mouth.

SOLD TO THE KING

With jerking spasms, he unloaded his hot load, then slowly released his grip on my head. As he pulled out, the last spurt of royal cum landed on my lips. He rubbed the dripping head of his cock on the top of my pale breasts, still heaving as I caught my breath.

"Elva," he smiled with a dreamy look. "Thank you."

I looked at him, tears welling in my eyes. I had pleased the King and not sacrificed my purity. All my life, I had been taught to respect and love the King.

And now I had done just that.

"I have decided on your future, Elva."

He held my chin and looked down at me, his cock, still hard and wet near my face.

"You will become first-wife to my oldest son, Shane. And one day, when he becomes King, you shall be the Queen of the Braeyork Dominion, all of the Passview Western Territories and the Channel Islands of Highbridge."

4

AIDEN

News that Elva was to be betrothed to my brother Shane as his first-wife travelled quickly through Braeyork Castle. When it reached my ears, in the stable grooming my headstrong black mare Champian, I howled in anger.

The startled horse threw up her head and neighed loudly, straining against the bridle. I patted her sturdy neck and tried to calm her, but her grunts and shivers continued.

"Shhhhhh," I whispered, rubbing the patch of soft white hair running down the bridge of her coal-black nose. "I feel the same. Elva deserves better."

Champian lowered her head. I saw my reflection in her brooding brown eyes. "There's nothing I can do," I explained. "The betrothal is tonight. And Shane chose me as his Virum Optimum."

I shook my head in disbelief.

Shane wanted me as his best man? The thought of performing the duties of the Virum Optimum, supporting my brother through the marriage ceremony, and even worse, serving as one of the witnesses to the first mating of his virgin bride...

"No!" I gasped. My brother is not worthy of her. She will be nothing more than a womb to produce heirs for the Braeyork Dominion. Shane will not hesitate to take a second and third-wife and continue his regular visits to the King's stable of exotic fuck dolls.

I hung my head as I led Champian to the open pasture and released her into the open field. I had not lost Elva to Shane. She had never been mine.

And now, she never would be.

When I arrived at the betrothal ceremony that evening, dressed in the dark gold-trimmed uniform of the Royal Braeyork Defenders, the company of elite guards under my command, I worried how I could hide my anger from Shane and my broken heart from Elva. I was not the type of man who easily hid his feelings.

As part of the ceremony in my role as Shane's Virum Optimum, it was my duty to walk the maiden to be betrothed up to the front of the hall past the assembled guests where the High Meister, the groom, and the King would receive her.

I stood near the back of the room, waiting for Elva's arrival. When the wooden doors opened, and she slowly approached, flanked by her lady-in-waiting, I silently cursed the gods who allowed Shane to be born a minute earlier than me. If I were Prince of Crasmere, heir to the throne, Elva would be my one and only wife, the future Queen of Braeyork, and more importantly, the queen of my heart forever.

She slowly glided toward me with her long flaxen white hair falling behind her. She was dressed in a lacy, tightly-fitted ivory gown, straining to contain the two round globes of her fleshy breasts. I tried not to stare, but it was difficult with such a vision of perfection only a few feet away from me.

Draped in the middle of both arms, she wore the traditional *palliolum.* The silky red material hung all the way to the floor, a symbol of long life and fertility. Her face was covered with a veil of translucent tulle fabric, affixed to her hair with white orchid buds. The back of the thin veil trailed behind her as a long train.

I held my breath as she approached. My face flushed and grew hot. Blood pounded to my loins. As Elva was presented to me, her lady-in-waiting raised her veil. It was my duty to greet her with a kiss on each cheek. Her eyes widened as I stepped closer.

I could almost taste her jasmine and lily fragrances on my lips. My body grew stiff, standing so close to her. I fought my desire to wrap her in my strong arms, kiss her deeply, and let our bodies meld together as one being. My cock throbbed, straining inside my tight trousers.

"Elva," I trembled as I bent closer to kiss her cheek, "you are an angel. I am here for you, and I always will be."

"Thank you, Aiden," she replied. Our eyes found each other in that briefest of moments, staring as if we suddenly knew that our souls would never know peace if we were not together, and yet crushed knowing we never could be.

I kissed each soft cheek, my lips lingering just a second longer than I should as a good brother-in-law to be. The mere touch of her milky white skin to my lips, with my arm around her slender waist, caused my cock to bulge. I had never felt such a raw, primal urgency. I squeezed my legs against my growing desire. The outline of my stiff member must have been obvious to anyone who glanced down at my trousers.

We slowly walked the aisle, arm-in-arm, as is the custom of betrothed and Virum Optimum. Those gathered to watch the ceremony smiled and nodded their heads as we made our way to the front, where the King, my brother Shane, and the High Meister waited.

Holding Elva's arm in mine, feeling her so close as we walked in perfect unison, I let myself imagine she was mine. I would bed her tonight and every night. I would love her today and every day. We would grow old together, raise children and spoil our many grandchildren.

And never *ever* fall out of love.

My father, King Rolfe, beckoned us forward as we reached the stone altar. Elva and I stopped. I turned to her and bowed my head. "Forever," I whispered, "I will always be your protector."

She didn't reply, but her face seemed cast in anguish. I stepped away after presenting her and took my place beside Shane. His vacuous, leering gaze at Elva both saddened and angered me.

How could the gods have pushed him from my mother's womb before me?

~

After the betrothal ceremony, Elva left the hall with her lady-in-waiting and with the other women in the hall. I followed Shane toward the closed doors of another reception. My father had invited his harem of fuck dolls to party with the men while their wives went to gossip with the King's first-wife Ursula in the Ambrosia ballroom at the far corner of Braeyork Castle.

I stood watching Shane, who only a few minutes earlier had taken the solemn betrothal oath to Elva to become her husband. Now he stood with a naked young fuck doll by his side, laughing and drinking a foaming glass of ale.

Thoughts of Elva played in my mind. I felt ashamed at how easily I had fallen for her, like a schoolboy smitten with first love. I wanted her in every possible way. Try as I might, I could not rid myself of the image of her perfectly sculptured body nor the soft feel of her smooth, innocent face. The fragrance of her perfume lingered with every breath I drew.

My lust and my love were absolute. I knew I must rid myself of such desire and feelings for my brother's future first wife.

"Prince Aiden," a voice purred in my ear. I glanced over at a shapely young fuck doll dressed in a tight leather bodice pushing her ample breasts tightly together. "Is it true what they say about you?"

I smiled, even though I disapproved of using my father's harem. I knew the gossip about me amongst the fairer sex of Braeyork Castle, the whispers about my 'size.' Before I could respond, the fuck doll dropped her hands to the front of my trews, tracing the outline of my cock.

"I'm Donassa," she whispered into my ear with her wet lips, "your brother asked me to 'look after you' tonight."

I responded to Donassa's touch against my will. She loosened my belt and reached inside my pants for my stiffening cock. I closed my eyes as her long fingers stroked the shaft and then wrapped them completely around my aroused manhood.

"It *is* true," Donassa purred, stroking slowly, letting her soft fingers gently massage the full length and girth. "How does anyone take all of you?"

I opened my eyes to see the face of this fuck doll. Donassa was about my age, with dark hair and glistening lips. Though it was Elva I craved, my cock was in the skilled hand of this nearly naked temptress. I needed release from the ache that had been building up from being so near to Elva for the last hour.

I moaned as Donassa continued to stroke me, her fingers paying special attention to the engorged head. She smeared cum leaking from the tip of my cock over it and slowly teased the full length as she pulled down my black trews with her other hand.

Donassa dropped to her knees in front of me. She looked up, smiling as she reached behind her back and undid her bodice. It dropped to the ground, freeing her breasts from their tight confines. She pressed them together with her hands, forming an inviting gap between them.

"Do you want to fuck them, Prince Aiden?" Donassa raised herself up from her knees and wrapped her tits against my pulsating cock. She spat on it and rubbed her saliva over the tip.

I grunted as she rocked herself up and down, sliding my slicked cock head between her soft breasts. I slowly fucked her generous cleavage, and with each upward thrust, the tip of my cock got closer and closer to her red-glossed lips.

I thrust myself between her tits, pressing my cock close to Donassa's lips. She flicked her tongue over it. Cum was rising in my balls as I closed my eyes again and saw the face of the one I desired so fiercely.

Elva.

I saw her face as I silently spoke her name. I thrust over and over between the soft opening of the fuck doll's tits. If I did not have Elva, I would have no reason to live. I needed to possess her and to be possessed by her. Our bodies were born to fuse together in everlasting love.

Donassa stopped fucking my cock with her tits. I opened my eyes as she grinned and then, without another word, opened her lips and took the head of my cock inside her warm mouth.

"Ohhhhh," I groaned, closing my eyes again. I pulled Donassa's head closer and pumped my fat cock into her mouth, though she could only take the first couple of inches. My balls tightened.

I needed to be inside of Elva, to open her completely. I thrust my cock deep into Donassa's mouth; as my cock stiffened, I could no longer hold back. I held her head as I released into her mouth, jerking and spasming until cum dripped from her mouth and fell onto her milky tits.

I am yours, Elva.

I spoke the words silently as the fuck doll Donassa washed my cock head with her tongue, ropes of cum still dripping from her mouth.

"Thank you," I said, wishing I had not demeaned her in such a fashion. I offered her my hand, helped her up to her feet and whispered. "Come and see my regent at the stables tomorrow. I will leave a bag of coins for you to find a better life."

She looked confused. "Your royal highness?"

"I think you can be more than a fuck doll," I told her. "Pursue a new avenue. Find your purpose and someone worthy of you."

With a bow, Donassa whispered, "Thank you, Prince Aiden." She grabbed her bodice, lying in a heap beside her, and scurried away. I watched her head toward the side entrance, turning and nodding to me one more time before she exited.

I pulled up the trousers of my uniform and glanced around to see my brother Shane a few feet away from me, thrusting into the pussy of a curvaceous fuck doll. He pumped a few times and then stopped.

"I want your asshole," he commanded.

The poor girl cowered before him. "Please, Your Royal Highness, I am too small."

Shane grunted. "Vanessa!" he shouted. "Bring your ass over here."

I watched in disgust as a heavier fuck doll hurried over to Shane. She danced, stripped for him, and then positioned herself on all fours like a dog waiting to be mounted.

Shane spat on her asshole, gliding his cock over it before pushing forward, slowly easing himself into her ass. Without giving her time to adjust, he wrapped his fingers around her hips, thrusting into her quickly and roughly. Her breasts swayed back and forth with the movement, his hands pulling her body back to meet his.

His thrust grew frenzied, and his face screwed up as he neared his release, burying himself into her and grunting like a farm animal as he came inside her. And then, after a moment, Shane smacked her ass and sent her away.

It was hard for me to accept that someday my brother would rule the Braeyork Dominion. I approached him as he pulled on a robe, and a fuck doll with a red-painted body poured him another glass of wine.

"I'm leaving," I told him.

"So soon, brother?" he laughed. "I wanted you to help me select a second-wife from..." he swept a hand around the room at the fuck dolls—some dancing provocatively and others servicing guests, "father's little harem."

"You're going to take a second-wife?"

"Of course," he chuckled. "And a third as well. As is my right and my duty, brother."

My stomach churned. "What about Elva?"

"Father chose her, and I concur. She will bear handsome sons and beautiful daughters." Shane motioned to one of the scantily dressed fuck dolls holding a tray of fruit and sweets. "She will soon be with child and too fat to be much use in bed."

"You are not worthy of her," I retorted. "Elva deserves to be your one and only wife. She is all the woman you need."

Shane laughed as the fuck doll fed him a grape. He squeezed one of her tits through her lace blouse before shooing her away. He slurped some of the wine, spilling it down his chest, then turned to me, anger flashing in his eyes.

"You do as you please, brother, but keep your foolish ideas of mounting only one wife to yourself." Shane snarled. "Or I'll make sure you have no wife at all."

5

ELVA

T he soft bed filled with down goose feathers was a luxury I had never before experienced. The morning after my betrothal, I awoke in the largest and most comfortable bed I had ever laid upon.

The mountains of plush blankets and the endless bounty of soft pillows left me in awe. That such a world of comfort and warmth existed anywhere in Braeyork left me breathless. I slept naked under the satin sheets. It was much too warm inside my cozy cocoon to cover my body with clothes.

Creena, my lady-in-waiting, assigned by King Rolfe after my visit to his chamber, explained that I would have a few weeks to prepare for my wedding to Shane, the Prince of Crasmere and the future King of the Braeyork Dominion. During those weeks, my every need would be attended to by Creena. I was also assigned a dresser, a hair stylist, a tutor, and a group of women who would help with bathing and any other task to which I assigned them.

Someday, I would be the Queen of Braeyork. I had much to learn.

I was not sure I needed such doting care and extravagant luxury, but for this morning at least, as I lay waking in this gilded room in a canopy bed, I was thankful for the chance to have a few moments to myself.

"The Prince looked so handsome last night," I heard a young female voice whisper.

I tried to peek at the speaker. She was a girl, about my age, with a feather duster in hand going about the chamber. Beside her stood two other girls, perhaps just a little younger. One carried towels, and the other poured a steaming bucket of water into a tub, presumably for my morning bath.

I felt a little self-conscious, naked under the sheets. I kept my eyes closed, hoping they would think I was still sleeping.

"And *she* was so beautiful," another girl added. "Queen Elva. I love saying that! It sounds *soooo* perfect. Oh my, what a match the King has made for Prince Shane!"

Despite myself, I smiled at their compliments. Shane did indeed present a dashing form last night. I should feel lucky that I would soon be his wife.

"But did you see his brother, walking her down the aisle?" A young voice spoke in tones of adulation. "Was it just me? I swear it looked like he wanted her even more than his brother!"

All the girls laughed. "Oh, we saw it. He couldn't hide that monster if he tried!"

The giggling girls almost made me laugh too. I held my mouth, trying not to give myself away.

"And she seemed so happy in Prince Aiden's arms. Can you imagine those two together?" a girl with a huskier voice added. "I felt a thrill just thinking about them, kissing and touching…. and well, you know what!"

I was getting hot under the sheets listening to such frank talk. I had not noticed Aiden's 'excitement' for me. But the memory of his kiss on my cheek, his strong arms around me as we walked, and his warm breath promising to be there for me, be there forever—all flooded my senses.

A damp urgency was growing between my legs. I pressed my bare knees together, saying Aiden's name softly to myself, remembering his lips upon my face.

I squeezed my thighs together as tightly as I could.

"Is it true what they say about Prince Aiden?" The girl with the husky voice whispered.

"I saw him once," another replied, "when I was sent to bring fresh linens after his bath. I surprised him. When he rose up, I got a good look. Even soft, he is as big as the white stallion in the barn!"

I moaned at their crude talk. Aiden was so gentle yet so strong. As the girls kept talking and giggling, I reached for the rosebud between my legs. The King called it my 'clit.' I touched it gently, imagining Aiden doing the same to me with his tongue or his large calloused fingers.

My excitement grew as I circled the bud and the hood with my finger, wetting it with the dampness of my pussy. I clenched my eyes as I rubbed my clit. Aiden was holding me, possessing me, and finally, inside of me, filling me up so fully... so completely... so perfectly.

My body convulsed as I felt myself quiver and cum—once, twice, and then yet again. I muffled my screams as waves of pleasure rolled through me until I was completely spent with the thought of belonging to Aiden.

L ater that day, after I was bathed, groomed, and dressed by my little army of attendants, I sat across from my future husband and his brother Aiden at the long linen-covered dining table of King Rolfe and his new first-wife, the copper-haired Ursula. She was not that much older than me, her belly swollen with a new child for the King. Apparently, the baby was due in a little over four months, sometime this winter, early in the new year.

We were joined for the mid-day meal by the pompous High Meister, Zachron, seated directly beside me. I tried to avoid his eyes, thoughts of our foul encounter still fresh in my mind. When he did glance at me, leering with a dark, cunning smile, I clenched my jaw and looked away. I knew too much of his disgusting nature.

If I ever gained any leverage in court, he was the first person I would replace. Perhaps time serving the King in the never-ending night of the frozen Barrenlands would be a fitting end to his career.

When the first course of oyster bisque and potato flatbread was served, I dipped my spoon into the creamy soup. The spicy yet delicate flavors of the soup were unlike anything I had ever tasted growing up in tiny provincial Saxcoate.

"Mmmm," I sighed contentedly after taking a second spoonful and a bite of the warm, buttered flatbread. Only Aiden seemed to notice my delight.

"The oysters were gathered and shucked this morning," he smiled, "while you were still in bed."

I flushed at the memory of pleasuring myself under the satin sheets. "They infuse it with such a delightful brine," I replied. "And yes, I'm afraid I did not rise with the rooster as usual. I was…"

I stopped myself, wishing I could share the truth with him. "I was rather preoccupied, that is I mean, quite tired from last night's ceremony."

His rugged face framed his wide smile as he combed thick fingers through his mane of long black hair falling around his dark face. It seemed like he was grooming himself for my eyes only. As I watched, the room grew warmer. I pressed my legs together, fighting the empty ache between them that had suddenly returned.

Aiden was about to reply to me when the King stood up. "I would like to offer my congratulations to Shane," he proclaimed, holding his full wine glass high in the air, "and, of course, to you, Elva. Welcome to our family."

Everyone raised their glasses to the King's toast. "Thank you, your Grace," I managed to respond after taking a sip of wine. "I am very honored."

Shane smiled at me, cocking his head like he had won the prized calf at the autumn fair. I glanced over at Aiden. He raised his eyes upward, shaking his head.

"Your grace, we should choose a date for the wedding," Zachron said as he set his glass down. "If we act quickly, you may welcome your first grandson in the spring."

"My thoughts exactly," King Rolfe replied. "How soon can it be done?"

Ursula, sitting at the corner of the linen-draped table, folded her hands in front of her. Our eyes met, and I could read tired resignation in her dispirited eyes. Her child would be the aunt or uncle of my baby, and if I were to bear a boy, my son would be next in line for the throne of the Braeyork Dominion.

"In two weeks, my Grace," the High Meister said, "on the seventh evening of the Fortnight of Crow. If I start now, I can have the Stone Temple readied for the ceremony," he paused, glancing suggestively at me. "The wedding party can return here by carriage for the celebration feast. And afterwards, of course, in your private chambers, we will sign the documents of consummation once we verify the first mating has been satisfactorily carried to… its happy climax."

A heavy fist pounded down on the table.

"No!" Aiden bellowed. "No!"

I turned toward him. His nostrils flared as he talked.

"To marry during the Fortnight of Crow is blasphemy!" He glanced over me and then fixed his gaze squarely at the King.

"Father, you know better than any of us. The Serpen Queen's evil peaks during the fourteen days of Crow. Any marriage during the fortnight will create an unholy match. It will be cursed by her evil."

King Rolfe sat down. All my life, I had heard tales about the Serpen Queen. The Fortnight of Crow, the two weeks preceding the start of the autumn harvest, was considered a time for hard work during the day and prayers to the gods at night. Almost every year, some disaster during Crow was blamed on the Serpen Queen's black magic.

"Those are peasant superstitions," Zachron interjected, lecturing the King. "The Serpen Queen was vanquished long ago. The same as the Vaeler usurper Dylan thanks to the bravery of Queen Pantaka, the mother of Shane and Aiden, who would surely want her oldest son to marry without the old fears."

I knew only vaguely the story of Pantaka. They called her the 'Warrior Wife.' But over the years, most of us had forgotten the details of her heroic death saving King Rolfe. I watched as the King whispered something to Ursula, the only other first-wife he had taken since the death of Queen Pantaka so many years ago.

Ursula shook her head.

"My wife disagrees High Meister, but I think it is time we put old myths to rest. We will proceed with the wedding in two weeks' time," the King confirmed. "We will not submit to fear."

"Father, I beg you, no!" Aiden had remained standing all this time.

He glanced over at me. Our eyes locked together momentarily before he turned back to face King Rolfe.

"They say that during Crow, the Serpen Queen can assume any form she desires, either human or animal. She could wreak havoc on the marriage ceremonies and infiltrate the assembly of nobles. She could poison the future of the whole Braeyork Dominion."

"Nonsense!" Zachron hissed. "You've been listening to too many tall tales. That is what happens when a Prince spends more time with peasants and the new recruits of his guard than with men of his own rank at the King's court!"

"And you will find out what happens when you ignore the wisdom of the past," Aiden replied, his commanding voice forcing Zachron to cower. "Your ignorance will ruin not only my family but the future of the entire realm."

"Enough, Aiden!"

King Rolfe stood up and took the hand of Ursula, pulling her up from the table. "My wife needs to rest. Zachron, begin the preparations for the wedding ceremony at the Stone Temple. I will instruct my steward to prepare for a grand feast in Braeyork Castle, the likes of which have not been seen in a generation."

The King covered Ursula's hand with his. "And Aiden, you will fulfill your role as your brother's Virum Optimum. After the reception, you, me and the High Meister will serve as witnesses to the first mating and legal consummation of the marriage of Shane and Elva. After which, they will be legally joined together in an unbreakable bond of royal matrimony."

King Rolfe turned to me and then back to Aiden. "Our legacy will live forever."

6

AIDEN

My father was the King of the Braeyork Dominion, ruler of the vast territories of Braeyork stretching all the way west to the Passview and south to the Sea of Tenebrise, including the Channel Islands of Highbridge. And to the north, the Barrenlands and the boiling peat swamps at the foot of the Bondoun crater were all under his control as well.

But he was not the ruler of me.

Or so I told myself the morning after the dinner to welcome Elva to our family.

"You and your brother will ride with me to Misty Loch this morning," the King informed me when I arrived at Braeyork Castle to inspect the guards under my command.

"Misty Loch?" I grumbled. It was a three hour ride north through marshy ground and rocky terrain. "Why? What's all the way up there?"

"Philip of Hart," my father replied, "the Chief of all the Harts in Rochford Province. The nobles of Rochford have sworn undying fealty to him and also…"

He hesitated momentarily, mounting his chestnut steed. "And his daughter, Marion is now of age to wed."

"But Shane's already…" I stopped myself, realizing what my father was planning. "No! Father, please!"

"Let's ride, Aiden," he replied. "We have a long journey ahead."

He turned to my brother, already seated on his horse, looking bored but compliant with our father's request to join him today. "Shane, help me explain the way of the world to your brother."

With a snap of his leather switch, the King's steed trotted off, and I reluctantly followed behind as a dutiful son.

There was nothing wrong with Marion. But there was everything wrong with me.

"A first wife is not unlike a gold bar, a thing of tremendous value and beauty, a source of prestige and power," Shane explained to me as we rode. "A union with the Harts will secure the loyalty not only of Philip, but of all the nobles in Rochford who bow to him."

"I will not marry someone I do not love," I pleaded with my father.

My father laughed. "You will have plenty of time for that. Perhaps not with your first-wife, which no one really expects anyway, but more likely with someone else who might come along. Second-wives are unusually fond of being the object of romantic infatuation."

Arguing was useless, I quickly realized. But I was puzzled. If a first-wife was a means of forging alliances and consolidating power, why was Elva chosen to marry Shane? Marrying her offered no political advantage.

My father grinned at my question as we arrived at Hart Castle in time for the mid-day feast. "She is the rarest of beauties. The finest mares are bred to enhance the bloodline of the stallion."

His reply rang in my ears as I studied Marion, sitting at the end of the long table beside her father, Philip of Hart. If Elva was selected as a breeding mare for our family, then Marion, extremely pretty but somewhat meek and withering, was more a golden goose.

And I nothing more a gander on a leash.

Marion and I walked alone through the grounds of Hart Castle as our fathers and my brother stayed inside, planning our futures.

"I will be honest with you, Marion," I explained as we found a spot to sit overlooking the manicured gardens of her father's estate on the edge of the glassy waters of moody Misty Loch. "I would be a poor choice for you. My heart, I am afraid, is smitten with another."

She pouted her lips, releasing a tiny sigh. "Oh."

"I have dreams and goals," I spoke softly, trying not to cause her undue discomfort. "And I'm not suited to the custom of taking a second and third-wife. I am a foolish romantic, I know. I seek but *one* wife, a true companion in every aspect of the word."

"I do not think you foolish," Marion replied. "But you are certainly naive. I know my duty, and I do not care to torture myself with the type of illusions you espouse. Our union will serve our families. After we are married, you are free to seek what you need with anyone you choose. It was the same for my mother and her mother before her. I will produce heirs and raise our family. If by chance we find the type of companionship you desire, I will be satisfied, dare I say, even happy."

She held my eye. "But I will not be crushed if we do not."

Before I could reply, she rose from the chair. "Prince Aiden, you are a son of the King. I look forward to the honor of becoming your first-wife and serving the Braeyork Dominion."

She touched the top of my head and left me staring as she walked away and wandered into the shrubbery of the ornamental gardens.

After the feast of roasted quail and wild boar, a tour of the paddocks where barded war horses in full armor pranced to my father's delight, the men all retired to a large drawing room in the depths of Hart Castle.

The women, including Marion and Philip of Hart's first-wife, Georgina, left us. The heavy doors of the ballroom were sealed shut the moment the women departed.

I wasn't sure exactly what my father and Philip had decided about my future with Marion, but by the manner in which they laughed and drank their Black Brandy, I surmised they had agreed on terms.

"Now," Philip exclaimed as he set down his empty glass. "Do you wish to see the other beauties of Hart Castle?"

"Indeed we do!" my father boomed.

Beside Philip stood a man of advancing age who introduced himself.

"Your Grace, King Rolfe," he bowed a head to my father. "I am Erasmus, chancellor and advisor of Philip. As you may know, all seven of the noble families of Rochford, the finest horse breeding and husbandry province in Braeyork, have pledged fealty to my Lord, Philip the Third of Hart, son of Philip the Second."

Erasmus was a tall, graying, lanky sort of man with darting black eyes and thin lips. He held his head high with a sense of pompous prestige. I cared not for the feeling he instilled within me as he continued to extol the virtues of his 'Lord.'

"And along with their undying fealty to Philip has come an abundance of pecuniary riches," Erasmus explained. "My Lord has wisely directed me to use some of his wealth to acquire a harem of fuck dolls. And while we dare not claim to challenge the superiority of your harem, my Grace," he bowed again to my father, "they do provide much comfort to my Lord and those upon whom he favors and as–"

"Yes, yes," Philip interrupted. "Let the girls in! Our guests are only here for a few hours."

"Of course, my Lord." Erasmus signalled a man in uniform standing at the door. The man nodded, turned and opened the heavy wooden doors. Five women rushed in and gathered at the feet of Philip as if they were his obedient pets.

"Gentlemen," he smiled as he gazed down at the scantily dressed entourage of female flesh. "Enjoy the variety of Rochford's finest fuck dolls. I am sure they are already wet and excited to serve you."

The women cooed at Philip, and he patted two of them. I felt disgusted by this display, and though one of the women caught my eye – a tall, dark-haired beauty, I vowed not to partake of their comforts.

Before I could excuse myself, my brother Shane rose up, his face flushed. I knew he had consumed a great deal of wine and now nursed a glass of Black Brandy.

"I would like to propose a toast before I get my cock sucked," he smiled, pointing to the same dark-haired woman who had caught my eye, "to my little brother, Aiden and to his promised first-wife, Lady Marion."

Marion may have accepted her fate without protest, but I would not. "Father," I hissed under my breath. "I will not marry her!"

Though I intended my words to be private, they echoed through the hall.

Shane scoffed. "Lord Philip, my brother is a man of fanciful ideas. He will be glad to accept the hand of your daughter, and my Father and I will grant you most favored status for commerce and grant any titles you might wish to bestow upon your nobles."

Philip nodded but looked concerned. He glanced over at me. "Prince Aiden, you and my daughter will make a fine match. Your children... grandchildren I will share with the King, will want for nothing."

"Yes, Lord Philip," I replied. "Lady Marion is a rare beauty, and I know she will make a fine wife. But, I'm afraid, not with me."

"Aiden!" Shane spat. "Outside. Now!"

"**Y**ou selfish prick!"

My brother's face reddened as he lashed out the moment the heavy doors closed behind us.

"Selfish?" I glared back at him. "For standing my ground?"

"For your daft, fucking stupidity! For putting yourself above the Crown and Braeyork, above even our own Father!"

Shane stepped closer, nostrils flaring. We often fought as children growing up, and I, always a little bigger and heavier, could easily triumph in any skirmish. But rather than hurt him, I usually allowed him to win.

He was, after all, the heir – and I the spare.

But we were no longer children. He was my brother, and I loved him, but I would not allow him, or anyone else, to choose my wife.

"I am not a pawn on a chessboard," I finally responded.

"No. You are a knight, second in line to the throne. Your duty is to be ready to assume the Crown if I falter before I produce an heir." Despite the amount of drink he had consumed, Shane spoke firmly.

"I lead the Royal Braeyork Defenders," I countered. "My men and I are sworn to protect the King and Braeyork with our lives if necessary. And I am sorry, but I alone will choose to whom I give my heart."

"Your heart?" Aiden shook his head. "No one cares who you give that to!"

"But—"

"It is your cock!" Shane interrupted. "That is what we care about, what is required of you. To whom will you give the gift of your princely cock? Aiden, brother, listen to me. The woman who will take your royal seed, the first wife whose children will forge an unbreakable political alliance to advantage the Crown – that is what is at stake here. That is where your duty lies."

"You think me disloyal because I seek to follow my own path?"

"I do indeed!" Shane's tone had turned from an angry threat to a reasoned argument. "You betray your responsibilities to the Dominion, to the glorious history of Braeyork. And worse, to the King, to our father."

I could not easily dispute his reasoning even though I cared not to propagate the customs of a land that subjugated so many for the benefit of so few, a system that bestowed privilege upon men to choose and women to follow. But I also did not want to disappoint my father. I had pledged to serve the King and protect the Dominion of Braeyork with my life if necessary.

Still, I had to find a way to stay true to myself.

"So, what is it going to be, Aiden?" Shane gripped my shoulder firmly. "Brother?"

I marched back into the drawing room behind Shane. Silently, dutifully. Obediently.

The young ladies remained gathered around Philip's feet as everyone watched us take our seats.

Aiden raised his glass of brandy. "A toast. To the match of Prince Aiden and Lady Marion!"

The men raised a glass of brandy and drank. The ladies clapped politely.

There was nothing more I could do. If I could just accept the time-honored traditions of Braeyork, and the customs of my royal family, I would have a fine first-wife and be free to seek love wherever I might find it.

Alas, I would do no such thing.

After serving as Shane's Virum Optimum, and before my arranged marriage to Marion could take place, I would disappear and seek a new life far from Braeyork Castle.

"Now that we have settled that," my father proclaimed, beaming as everything unfolded as he had planned. "We'll plan for a spring wedding. Another royal wedding!"

Philip of Hart stood up and took the hand of two of the ladies. He led them both to me.

"Prince Aiden," he said stiffly. "You do me a great honor in taking my daughter as your bride. Please accept my gratitude with two of my best fuck dolls, Gillian and Peach."

I started to protest, but Philip had already turned and walked away. The two women, both stunning in appearance and tempting in their sheer lacy outfits, knelt down at my feet.

Philip distributed the remaining women to Shane and my father. The last woman took her place at Philip's feet. The debauchery was set to begin.

The strawberry blonde-haired woman to my left spoke. "I am twenty-one, and I'm sure you might be able to guess why I am called Peach."

She smiled, stood up and undid a clasp behind her neck. Her sheer gown fell to the floor.

I stared at the naked beauty standing before me. Her full red lips and the light blush of her cheeks gave her a sensual yet innocent demeanor. A silver necklace dangled between her small breasts. Her pussy was covered in reddish blonde hair, trimmed into the shape of a peach.

Though I vowed not to fuck her, my cock hardened at the sight of this desirable young creature.

Not to be outdone, her companion rubbed the calves of my leg, reaching high up my trousers toward my groin before pausing just below the outline of my protruding phallus.

"And I am Gillian, a year older than Peach… and so much more experienced, your royal highness."

I flinched as she glided her hand over my stiff cock. It ached against the restraining material of my trousers. Gillian batted her thick eyelashes at me. She was the dark-haired beauty that had caught my eye earlier. Where Peach's figure was somewhat slight, Gillian's was full and round. Her sumptuous breasts strained to be free of her tight-fitting black smock, the deep cleavage drawing my eye.

I fought the urge to fuck her creamy white tits as she slowly traced the outline of my cock imprisoned inside my trousers.

"You can have us both," Peach purred, gyrating before me. Gillian stood up and pulled her smock up and over her head, revealing her ample breasts, which she proudly displayed for my inspection. She pinched her surprisingly small nipples, and an idea began to form in my head.

"Peach," I said, "would you sit before me and let me watch you touch yourself? May I see your…" I tried my best to sound commanding, "*all* of your peach?"

"Oh, your highness!" Peach exclaimed. "It will be my honor!"

As she complied with my request, Gillian leaned closer. "And how may I service you, your royal highness? My pussy is so wet."

No. I was not going to fuck Gillian. But my throbbing cock demanded relief.

"Release the prisoner," I pleaded, "inside my trousers."

"Yes, your Grace!" She fell to her knees bare-chested, with only a thin chemise covering her thighs. She unbuckled my belt and reached her hand inside my trousers, feeling for my pulsating organ.

"Oh my!" she exclaimed as she wrapped her long fingers around it and pulled it out. "This is a grand royal cock, your highness." She teased the head with her fingers, and I groaned.

"Let me get you out of your trousers," she said, pulling them down around my boots so nothing would obstruct her. She knelt between my bare legs and slowly stroked the long thick shaft of my thickly veined cock.

"That's good, Gillian," I moaned. "Stroke it."

Peach, sitting on the chair, her legs spread, called out. "Oh fuck! I need that big cock inside me, your highness!"

"Mmmmm," I wanted that too, but I was determined not to yield to temptation. "Pleasure yourself, Peach. Let me watch you play. Touch yourself."

"Yes, your royal grace. Do you want to see me make myself cum?" She wet her finger in her mouth and held it between her lips. "For you?"

"Yes, please…" I moaned as Gillian lovingly stroked my cock, her long fingers sliding all the way up and down the shaft until she covered my shiny slick head, smearing drops of seed already leaking from the slit.

As Peach brought a finger down to her pussy lips, teasing herself with one hand and massaging one of her breasts with the other, I glanced over at Shane. He was pounding into a full-figured naked fuck doll from behind as if she were a dog. He held his drink in his hand and fucked her while sipping his brandy.

Beside him, my father had his fuck doll positioned on his lap, fucking her slowly while she shoved her tits into his mouth.

Philip of Hart and his advisor Erasmus watched the three of us while a single fuck doll serviced both of them with her mouth, alternating between their two cocks.

The scene was one of depravity, an orgy I did not condone, and yet here I was, enjoying the sight of Peach using her fingers to fuck herself while her companion stroked my cock. I might have lofty, high morals about such activity, but at the moment, I was no better than any other man in the room.

"Stroke me!" I yelled at Gillian. "Stroke my cock!"

"Yes, your grace. Cum for me!"

Gillian stroked faster and faster as I watched Peach use two fingers to fuck herself while she touched her clit with her thumb, humping up and down on the chair, her hips thrusting up to meet each one, her fingers burying themselves knuckle deep before coming out glistening.

We both began to cry out as I felt seed rising in my balls and the moment of release at hand.

"Cum, your highness!" Gillian urged, "all over me!"

She moved between my legs, and as Peach screamed out in pleasure, I spurted cum all over Gillian's face. As I continued to spasm, she tongued the head of my cock and then took all of it into her sweet, warm mouth.

I cried out from the pleasure of such exquisite relief.

And from the pain of hating myself.

7

ELVA

I was surprised by the handwritten invitation I received this morning. It was from the Queen, Ursula.

"*Dearest Elva*

We met but two days ago when you dined with us at Braeyork Castle, so excuse my boldness, but I request the honor of your company at tea this afternoon. A private tea for you and I.

Although I am your Queen, and soon, your mother-in-law, I hope we will be more akin to sisters... the two first wives of Braeyork Castle.

Please join me today if you are able. I have matters of some importance to discuss with you.

In love and admiration,

Ursula"

I read the note a few times, growing more perplexed each time. A private tea with the Queen? The two first wives of Braeyork Castle?

Of course, I would join Ursula. But first, my dressers would need to advise me as to what manner of clothes I should wear and how to present myself to her Royal Majesty the Queen.

S tanding before Ursula, the Queen of the Braeyork Dominion and all its territories, I should have been somewhat apprehensive. Instead, with a touch of her hand on my arm, I felt an instant kinship.

"Elva!" she purred with a smile as she held my arm. "I'm *so* glad you accepted my invitation. I fretted all day long that you might not have time for me."

"Time for you?" I replied with genuine surprise. "Your Majesty, it is a great honor to–"

"Please, please, call me Ursula," she interrupted, squeezing my arm. "All those titles make me sound so... so old and well..." she giggled, leaned in closer and whispered, "You know, really fucking stuck up!"

I laughed out loud and stared at this noble lady. Her copper-tinged hair was neatly arranged and pinned in a tight bun over her head. Her porcelain complexion, soft blue eyes, delicate nose, and high cheekbones suited her well, exactly how I had always envisioned the Queen of Braeyork might look.

SOLD TO THE KING

That was when she was the far away, distant Queen. But her direct manner endeared her to me immediately.

"That's quite fine, your maj..." I corrected myself mid-sentence, "Ursula."

"Come in, Elva, make yourself at home. We have all the finest pastries and teas you can imagine. I had the cooks prepare everything this morning, fresh... for you."

The guards who escorted me here had closed the doors after I entered, and now I took in the panoramic view of the manicured gardens below. The Queen's apartment chambers were a set of adjoining rooms for sitting, sleeping and dining. We sat across from each other in two large stuffed armchairs, both wide enough for two, maybe even three people.

Ursula sank into her chair. The round protrusion of her swollen belly held a tiny royal baby, and I was somewhat in awe of how she still managed to look as elegant as any woman I'd ever known.

"The baby is doing well?" I asked as I surveyed the table. A steaming pot of tea, sweet cakes, rolls, pastries, softened butter, clotted cream and all manner of colorful jams and jellies were arranged neatly over a pressed linen tablecloth. "When are you due?" I asked.

She leaned down and poured us both tea before she replied with a grunt. "The baby's fine. In the new year, the King will have his heir." She sighed. "Well, another heir, at least."

Her tone was decidedly sour. I reached for the cup of tea she had poured for me, dropped in a thin lemon slice and a cube of sugar. As I stirred it slowly, I wondered about the odd tone of her voice.

"Ursula," I began, weighing my words carefully. "You seem somewhat…"

"Pissed?" she smirked.

I giggled again, for the second time in the last few minutes. "Well, as a matter of fact, yes!"

She nodded, and her face tightened as she sipped her tea, all the while staring at me with a rather frightening intensity. She laid the cup down and reached for a pastry, smothering it with a dollop of cream. "Do you know the role of a first wife, Elva?"

"I think I understand. To bear children and to nurture them? To be a faithful partner to a husband?"

"Faithful partner?" She snorted out her tea at my answer.

I sipped my own tea. It was the smoothest I'd ever tasted, with just a perfect hint of lemony bitterness softened by the sugar. I was still trying to work out what I was doing here with this Queen who was so different than I had imagined.

"Faithful? While he is out fucking his second and third wife? Faithful? While he brags to his council about all his fuck dolls and how many of them have sucked his royal cock?"

Ursula spoke with unusual frankness for a Queen and in a stern tone that frankly scared me. But I also was beginning to guess why I might be here. Did she have anyone else with whom she could vent such frustrations?

"I know it's the privilege of nobles to do such things," I replied meekly. "But, are there not some benefits to being a first wife and the Queen of Braeyork?"

"Ahhh, yes, the benefits of being the Queen," Ursula nodded as she answered dryly. "I am loved by the King when we are seen together before the people. I am loved, they say, *by* the people. But, Elva, I've never known the kind of love that…"

She looked away, staring out the window at the gardeners busy pruning the lush rose vines and violet bushes, "the kind of love I read about in verse and prose by our great poets. It's a love that makes your heart beat faster, and your…"

Ursula bit her lip, closed her eyes and breathed in deeply before she finished her sentence, "And, excuse my direct language… love that makes your pussy moist!"

"Oh, yes, yes." I thought of Aiden when she spoke. He did exactly that to me. "The King told me I was as naive as a schoolgirl to think I could marry for love and save myself for a husband that would truly love me."

"The King told you that?" Ursula sat up. "After he bought you, did he not…" She stared at me blankly without finishing her thought.

"He did not open my petals if that is what you are wondering." I wasn't sure how much more to tell her. But I felt it was my duty, as another woman she had already confided in, to tell her the truth.

"The King allowed me to serve him," I felt my throat tighten, "in other ways."

Ursula smiled. "Thank you for being honest, Elva. I can see we're going to be good friends." She poured a little more tea into her cup. "Tell me, *how* exactly did you serve him?"

The room felt warmer as I recalled what I had done and what he had done to me. "I, I.. well, I sucked him after he stroked me and..."

"Did he make you cum?"

"Yes, with his fingers," I replied, feeling deep shame admitting such a thing to the King's first-wife.

"And you sucked his cock? You took his seed in your mouth?"

The frankness of her question surprised me, but she was the Queen. And not only was I her daughter-in-law to be, but I also felt a bond developing between us.

"Yes, I did. I'm very, very sorry, Ursula."

She stood up from the couch, holding the round ball of her stomach. "Elva, you have nothing to be sorry about. So, you are still a virgin?"

"Yes, ma'am, Ursula," I flustered. "I am."

"Come with me, Elva," she said as she headed toward a double glass door.

I followed her from the drawing-room where we had taken tea into a sumptuous bedroom chamber. A grand four-poster bed draped with sheer curtains dominated the room. She pushed aside the sheer material and sat on the bed.

"Come and sit." Ursula patted the bed. "Up here, beside me."

I couldn't help but feel a little better seeing her sitting on the bed and inviting me to join her. My sisters and I used to love the privacy of our tiny cottage bed whenever father was away. We played the silliest games, and the memory of those brief respites from our constant worries was something I dearly treasured.

$\sim$

Hopping up on the bed, I arranged myself near the Queen. My dressers had given me a frilly white blouse to wear, a long flowing dress and a short matching jacket.

The Queen undid the pins holding her hair and let it fall loosely around her head and shoulders. She looked at me a little peculiarly with something of a mischievous grin. "I was a virgin, too. I dreamed of marrying a man who would love me and I him, even if we were the poorest paupers in all of Braeyork."

"Instead, you married the richest man in Braeyork," I mused.

"Yes. Like you, my virginity was exchanged to benefit my family. In my case, so that my father and my brothers and uncles would gain the protection of the Crown and be favored with trading rights."

Her story echoed mine. My virginity was the only thing of value my father had ever possessed. But I was happy to trade it to help my whole family. They would not starve this winter. Thanks to me, their life of poverty was now but a painful chapter of the past.

"But Elva, I must tell you, being rich and having everything you thought you always wanted can be lonely. And so very frustrating. I have no one even to talk to most of the time."

"No!" I cried out. "Ursula, the King is a good man. Does he not take care of you and…" I stopped myself. The King had two other wives and a harem of fuck dolls. How much time did he spend with the Queen?

"Elva, the King has mounted me three or four times. Now that I am with child, he says it is no longer appropriate. I rarely see him."

Mounted? The word tasted bitter on my tongue.

"Mounted?" I repeated, holding my mouth, trying not to laugh.

"Yes," Ursula giggled and then spoke in a mocking voice imitating the King: "Spread your legs, wife. Your stallion is here."

"No!" I laughed. "Surely there was more to it than that?"

She shook her head back and forth. "No. A little cuddle, a few polite kisses and then he was off to his own chambers. Sometimes it feels like I am a doll on a shelf to be admired and then put away."

She removed her shawl and bunched up the long dress up around her waist until her bare legs were exposed. She folded her hands across her belly. "I know it's wrong, but I almost envy the King's fuck dolls. At least those dolls have fun!"

I smiled at her levity, but her description of the King troubled me. "Why is he so cold toward you, Ursula?"

"Guilt, I think," she replied, absently twirling a lock of her hair. "He loved his first wife, Queen Pantaka as many have told me. He never really got over her and only married me at the urging of his Inner Circle. They wanted another heir before the King got much older."

"But he seems so fond of you!"

She nodded. "He's a good man, loving and kind mostly, but his heart has never mended. His cock, though... well, that was never broken!"

We talked for a long time, both of us spreading out and getting comfortable on the bed as she told me more about her life. While her husband and all the noblemen of Braeyork found pleasure with multiple wives and frequent visits to the King's harem, first wives were expected to be chaste unto only their husbands.

"To be caught with a man other than your husband means your neck and the executioner's sword will not be long to kiss," Ursula explained.

I asked if there was anything I could do for her.

"Elva, after you marry Shane, I hope we can become the best of friends. I pray he gives you more attention than his father gives me."

I nodded, wishing I could just flee this place and take Ursula with me.

She studied me with wide eyes. "I do not wish to be forward, Elva, but your beauty is breathtaking." She leaned closer to where I lay propped up on the bed and touched my cheek. "You said the King asked you to serve him in *other ways*," she whispered.

"Yes," I replied, confused as to why she was asking me again.

"Would you ever consider serving your Queen?"

I left the Queens chambers one hour later. Her question had shocked me, but the tears in her defeated eyes haunted me. I said nothing at first as I considered how I could help her.

"Elva, some of the first wives, have found ways to…" she hesitated, "to bring a little joy to our lives."

I wasn't sure exactly what she wanted, but I had a pretty good idea. "You wish me to pleasure you?"

"Elva!" she replied with a scornful tone. "I do not give commands like the King. But if you must know, I ache to be touched, to be loved, to feel the type of pleasure that, yes, I know, is shameful for a Queen."

"No. Not shameful," I said. "You are a woman. You have needs. You are lonely. How can I serve you, my Queen?"

She smiled at my words and wiped away her tears. "Let me see you, Elva. All of you. And then, let me touch you. I have been thinking about this all day."

Ursula bit her lip. "I'm sorry, Elva. You must think me wicked."

I shook my head and slid off the bed. Slowly, I undressed before Ursula, removing the broach in my hair to let the flaxen curls unfurl around my head. She stared as I undid the clasps of my blouse and let it fall open, revealing my naked stomach and the deep valley between my breasts.

"You take my breath away," Ursula whispered, spreading her legs a little.

Opening my blouse, I displayed my naked chest to the Queen. She moaned a little at the sight of my young, firm bosom as I pinched my taut nipples.

"May I?" she groaned.

Nodding, I moved closer and climbed back on the bed. I fed my large breasts to her, and she sucked each one hungrily, moaning with the pleasure I was giving her. I pulled her head toward me and let her suckle my breasts until I began to feel my pussy tingle.

This was not something I had ever imagined, offering myself to another woman. But the joy I seemed to bring this lonely woman made me accept that such a blasphemous thing was not wrong.

"Now," I said, pulling back slowly. "Let me kiss you, my Queen."

Her wet eyes brightened, and without hesitation, I moved closer and pulled her head toward me. I kissed her on the lips tenderly. As she responded, I explored her mouth with my tongue. Her excitement and gratitude were obvious as she squeezed my breasts, kneading them as we kissed.

"Let me see more of you," she whispered after we had kissed for a long time. "May I taste you?"

"Yes," I replied. I stood up on the bed, unfastened the clasps of my skirt and let it fall around my legs. I stood on the bed in my linen chemise and moved my thighs close to her face. She touched me, rubbing her hand over my mound. I groaned in pleasure at her soft touch.

"You are so wet, my dear," she said, massaging the lips of my pussy through the chemise. She pulled it down to expose my blonde pussy. "Oh my, Elva. You are the most beautiful creature I've ever seen. More delicate than anything I could have ever imagined."

"Touch me," I whispered. "Taste me."

"Mmmmmm, yes," Ursula replied. Her fingers gently opened my pussy lips and rimmed around the entrance to my womanhood. Her knowing touch was slow and patient, and when she finally fingered my throbbing bud, I was on the verge of release. She leaned closer and kissed my clit with a feathery touch.

"Ohhhhhhhh, yessssss." A woman's kiss was so different. I couldn't help but grind my hips into her face. She began to lick my clit all around and under and then used her tongue to wash back and forth over it until I cried out. "Yes, make me cum!"

My knees buckled as I arched forward, waves of pleasure cascading through me as I began to cum all over the Queen's mouth. She held my hips as I screamed and bucked, riding out the pleasure until Ursula released her tongue and held my naked thighs in her arms.

She held me a long time until finally, I dropped down and sat beside her.

"Now," I said quietly. "Let me pleasure you, my Queen."

8

ELVA

During the next two weeks, as I prepared for my wedding in the little country cottage a good mile or so from Braeyork Castle, I rarely saw my future husband. My encounter with Ursula gave me a lot to wonder and worry about.

But really, what could I do about it?

All my life, I had heard stories about King Rolfe and the royal family, and like all my friends, I wondered about marrying Shane. As children, we were all taken with his good looks, his jovial manner, and all the 'gold' he must have hidden in his big castle.

A portrait of Shane standing with the King hung prominently in our place of worship. He was indeed a fine-looking man, but not really one who interested me. Of course, I always pretended I wanted the same as my sisters and friends – all starry-eyed maidens. But if truth be told, I never wanted to marry anyone. I didn't like the thought of being any man's wife.

Until I met Aiden.

I knew it was wrong to have such feelings. I was betrothed to his brother. I might be the Queen of Braeyork someday, with a young prince and a princess to raise. I could help my family back home in Saxcoate even more than I already had with the money, land, and animals that had been gifted to my father in return for my virginity.

I would be the Queen someday, the most powerful woman in the Braeyork Dominion, and my family would be forever protected. So then, why did I feel cheated? Was it because I was a nineteen-year-old who had never known love?

Would I become another Ursula?

I would be mated on my wedding night to a husband I barely knew, hoping that I would soon grow fat with his child in my womb. I knew it was my duty, and most girls would gladly trade places with me for the chance to marry the Prince of Crasmere, live a pampered life in Braeyork Castle, and someday become the Queen of a vast and prosperous dominion.

But my heart beat only for Aiden.

I knew I must let thoughts of him go, but every night when I closed my eyes, I saw his face. I tasted his musky odor on my lips, and I struggled to keep my fingers from touching my bud, imagining the instrument of his love plunging deep inside of me, filling me up as I imagined the thrill of belonging to him.

Aiden came by almost every day to see me, usually on his black mare, Champian. I helped water and groom the mare and listened to him describe his dreams of travelling to the western territories. He listened to my stories about growing up in Saxcoate and how I used to get into fights with just about everybody—boys and girls, men and women. He laughed at my jokes, and I at his, even though most were silly and some more than a little crude.

This afternoon, we walked slowly through the pasture, the soft autumn sunlight giving a glow to fields of golden grass swaying in the distance as far as the eye could see.

"After tomorrow, this will all be but a memory," Aiden said quietly.

Off in the pasture, Champian grazed free of saddle and reins. "Everything between us will change."

I had tried not to think too much about tomorrow when I would become wife to his brother. "Does it have to, Aiden?"

He stopped walking and bowed his head. "It must, Elva. You will move to Braeyork Castle, live with Shane, and bear his children. You will be more my sister than my…"

I could see the conflict on his face. Neither of us wanted to admit the depth of our feelings, to say out loud the truth of what lay within our hearts.

"Why…" I stammered, unsure of how to respond, how much to reveal of the desire for him that possessed me. After tomorrow, perhaps even today, such feelings were sinful and wrong.

SOLD TO THE KING

I turned and stepped closer, sweeping away a strand of my long hair. Aiden was so close. I touched his face, my palm resting on his beard, his head tilting. He drew me toward him, his strong hands around my waist, pulling me to him.

Our bodies pressed together, the comforting strength of his broad chest against my bosom, his bulging arms wrapping around me tightly like they could hold me forever, transporting us anywhere we wanted to go.

I laid my head on his shoulder. Tears filled my eyes. "Why," I repeated in a whisper, "why can we never be?"

He stroked my head gently. I could live happily in his arms, abandon myself to him completely, and live every day, every moment of my life, in the glow of his smile.

"It was not meant to be for us," he replied. "Tomorrow, you must forget all about me."

I released my hold and stepped back. His eyes were as wet as mine. "No, never!"

"You will belong to Shane, and you must, Elva. There is no other way."

My fists clenched together as I stood before him. "Is it true, Aiden? What Creena told me about Shane? He will breed me until I am with child and then take a second and a then third wife, and visit the King's harem too? You know him. Tell me, is that what he plans to do?"

Aiden did not reply. He drew slow breaths. His nostrils flared as he sucked in air.

"Tell me, Aiden!"

"My brother follows the customs of our father. And of his father before him, and of all the nobles in Braeyork. A first-wife is honored and kept holy, a mother to a man's heirs and heiresses." Aiden sighed, looking out over the pasture toward his mare. "Though I don't agree with the custom, I cannot speak ill of my brother. He will treat you well. You will want for nothing."

"I want for you!"

Aiden blinked, shaking his head as if refusing to accept the truth of the words I spoke. "After the wedding, Elva, and you are legally wed to Shane, I will leave Braeyork Castle and travel west, all the way to the Passview Western provinces past Goldenleaf."

He reached for my hands and squeezed them. "You must forget about me, and devote yourself only to my brother. Do you understand?"

"No!" I cried and threw myself at him, wrapping my arms around his middle and holding on tightly. He laid a hand on my head and let me cry until I was emptied of all my tears but not of all my sorrow.

"Princess Elva!" my lady-in-waiting Creena called out as I slowly awoke the next morning. Rays of warm September sunlight streamed through my bedroom window. She drew the curtains open wide. "Today is *the* day!"

I could only manage a dull moan. My life sentence was about to begin.

"You are a lucky woman, my Lady," Creena warbled. "Your world is about to change. Now, after your cake and tea, your bath should be ready. The ladies were up early, warming the water and mixing their wedding night perfume and bath oils."

The cakes tasted bland, and the tea ice cold as it plummeted down my gullet. But for the excitement of Creena and the other ladies, I would gladly have preferred to spend the day swilling pigs. Still, upon entering the warm bath, rich with wafting aromas of rose, hibiscus, and lavender, I felt my body relax a little.

Soft hands bathed and scrubbed me, massaged my scalp, and helped me wash my long white hair. As they worked, they peppered me with questions.

"Are you ready, my Lady, for…" a young girl giggled, her face flushing red, "for your first mating with the Prince?"

The girl seemed so excited. I smiled as I rose up from the bath. Towels were quickly wrapped around my head and body.

"Come, sit," Creena instructed, waving over an older lady, the beautician who applied makeup and powder. "You must be perfect for your husband."

Wrapped in only a fluffy towel, I sat down on a soft stool. Creena spread my bare legs apart for the beautician, who perched herself on her knees, sitting before me. With a soft brush, she combed the white hairs above the lips of my pussy, and with small scissors, trimmed each tiny hair. She dusted them with a fine powder and then spayed a mist of orange blossom oil over the lips of my womanhood.

"Tonight your petals will be spread for the first time," the beautician said as if revealing a great secret to me. "I want to be sure you are pleasing to his eye, perfect in every way when your husband enters you with his royal shaft and makes you his wife."

The young girls watching from a distance squirmed in near hysterics.

"Quiet!" Creena chastised. "A first mating ritual is a sacred act. Until it is completed and Prince Shane has released his seed within her womb, the marriage is not legal. All the witnesses must attest to the consummation and make their mark on the matrimonial register. It is no laughing matter."

The girls tried to hold their tongues, but I could see them smiling at each other, waiting to help dress me after my hair had been dried and styled.

Many hours later, I stood nervously, holding the arm of King Rolfe at the back of the Stone Temple. My long white hair had been curled in tight ringlets that dropped all the way down my back. My gown flared out from my narrow waist, falling to the floor in a long train behind me.

A lace shawl covered my bare shoulders. My silk wedding dress was fashioned in a way that accented the fullness of my breasts, snugly pressing against the stays sewn into my dress. It was a sign of my fecundity, Creena explained, a healthy, fertile bride for the Prince.

The white lace shawl and the blue Emerald Nuptiae necklace around my neck were symbols of my virginity. I was, in the eyes of everyone in the Stone Temple, the perfect companion for the future King of the Braeyork Dominion.

At exactly one minute after sunset, on the seventh day of the Fortnight of Crow, I began the slow walk to the front of the Stone Temple's great altar as a chorus of young voices began to chant the marriage hymn. The King and I glided down the aisle together ever so slowly.

I silently prayed to the gods to protect us from the Serpen Queen - so feared in my village, particularly during Crow. I remembered Aiden's warning, although no one else seemed worried. Perhaps they were right. It was a foolish old superstition.

I should not have let myself think about Aiden as I walked up the aisle. Just speaking his name in my mind made me tremble. When we took our final step to the altar and I caught my first sight of him in his dark blue uniform, standing tall beside Shane, my legs weakened. My perfumed pussy, bare under my gown as is the custom, begged to be his.

The King, dressed in royal furs and wearing his gold crown, kissed me on both cheeks, then took my hand and led me to Shane for the bridal inspection. Zachron, the High Meister conducting the marriage ceremony, took my hand from the King and removed my shawl. I was about to be presented as the herd's prized Heffer, I thought with disdain.

"Shane, Prince of Crasmere, heir to the throne of the Braeyork Dominion, all of the Passview Western Territories and the Channel Islands of Highbridge," Zachron spoke, loud enough to be heard by the entire congregation of more than three hundred souls, "the betrothed virgin is ready for your approval."

Shane smiled at me. His blonde locks had been neatly groomed. His white wedding vest, clean-shaven face, and bright manner were such a contrast to his brother standing beside him. Shane touched my cheek, ran a hand down my shoulder, and slowly walked around me, inspecting his prize. I realized it was all ceremonial, but I still burned at the shame of such a demeaning ritual.

"Do you approve of this woman who stands in her virgin purity before the gods and the congregation gathered here in this holy place?" Zachron barked.

"I do," Shane replied, his eyes twinkling at me.

I smiled, turning my head and searching for the eyes of another – his brother.

But Aiden looked straight ahead, holding his mouth tightly. He stood frozen at attention, ignoring me and everyone else in the Stone Temple.

9

AIDEN

I t was bad enough having to hold the ring in my pocket, but the thought of when I would hand it to my brother to place upon Elva's finger enraged me to depths of anger I had not realized existed within me.

As the foul-tongued Zachron had instructed me so carefully and with such libidinous glee, I would hand the wedding band of Alum gold only after we witnessed the successful climax of Shane and Elva's first mating.

"When the marriage is consummated, and his seed has been planted within her virgin womb," Zachron explained, "only then, will you hand over the ring, while she lays in the glow of her new husband's virility. And that will complete your responsibility as your brother's Virum Optimum."

I wasn't sure if I could stomach such a task and afterward make my mark beside the other witnesses—my father and the High Meister. Our marks on the marriage register would confirm that the marriage had been duly consummated and that Elva was forever bound to serve and obey her husband.

Bonds of matrimony in Braeyork could only be broken by the death of one of the spouses.

I watched Shane inspect Elva, but I would sooner be a marble statue than reveal the jealous anger festering within me. I hated myself for falling in love with her. Tomorrow I would be gone, and perhaps I could erase all memories of Elva from the torture chamber of my soul.

After the ceremony at the Stone Temple, I did my best not to look at her. It was much too painful, and I avoided her gaze.

But the reception at Braeyork Castle was a different matter. I fumbled my way through a toast to the bride and groom and had no choice but to glance over at her. I could not read her thoughts, but did I see a deep sadness in her drooping emerald eyes?

Or, was it only me, transferring my despair onto her and seeing what I thought should be written upon her face?

"And now," my father announced, standing up from the banquet table, glass in hand after the meal of roasted meats gave way to trays of sweet cakes and fruit, "it is time for the dances."

I had forgotten all about that custom. A bride danced in turn with her new father-in-law, the Virum Optimum, and then, finally, her husband. I watched as Elva and the King danced to the accompaniment of the stringed players. After they finished, it was my turn.

SOLD TO THE KING

Elva was presented to me by my father. "Your new sister-in-law," he beamed, "the future Queen of Braeyork."

I bowed. "My lady," I said stiffly and then raised my hand. She placed hers in mine, the contrast so soft and delicate. I drew her close to me, waiting for the music to begin.

"Why?" she whispered as we stared at each other, standing on display in the middle of the great hall, surrounded by hundreds of guests. "Why do you forsake me?"

The music began. I pulled her close, feeling the curves of her firm body pressing tightly against my wide chest. "I'm sorry, Elva. I died tonight. Forgive me, I mean you no disrespect."

The music carried us around the room. We moved as though we had danced together a thousand times. In fact, we had never done so before. I felt my cock stiffen in my uniform. I cursed my excitement as I tried to keep from pressing too close to Elva.

But she pushed her thighs between mine as the dance slowed. I worried I might explode, with only the thin material of my trousers separating the pulsing head of my cock from the lips of her naked pussy I knew lay but a hair's breadth beneath her wedding gown.

"Take me with you," she whispered, nearly touching my lips with hers. "We can escape tonight. Run away together, and that ring in your pocket will find its true purpose."

The suggestion made me shudder. I should pull her hips close to mine, lift her gown, and plunge my throbbing manhood into her deeper than any groom had ever taken his bride. This should be our wedding night.

But that was impossible. I would not betray my family, my brother, or my King.

Even for the only woman who had ever captured my heart.

"No, Elva," I replied. "Shane will put the ring on your finger. You belong to him."

The dance ended, and I bowed again politely as I saw Shane approaching from the corner of my eye. I stole a glance at Elva. She wiped tears from her eyes and then stood up straight and stiff, waiting to dance with her new husband.

I shuffled back a few steps as Shane came forward and tried to take his bow. He stumbled and fell to the floor. I hurried forward, worried that all the wine he had been drinking had stolen his balance.

"Brother," I whispered. His eyes were bloodshot, and a sheen of sweat glistened on his face. "Are you drunk?"

"No!" he chortled in the playful manner Shane always displayed. "I lost my footing. But the room has grown so warm, has it not?"

I helped him to his feet, and soon, he took his place with Elva. The wedding song began to play, and as I watched them dance, I tried my best to bury my feelings for his wife, though I knew it would take years, if ever, before I could find solace without Elva.

But as they danced and I studied Shane more closely, I couldn't help but notice a faraway look in his eyes and bands of moisture on his brow and lips.

My thoughts turned away from Elva.

I sensed an air of evil festering in Braeyork Castle.

10

ELVA

T his couldn't really be happening; I kept telling myself as I lay naked on the King's bed. The wedding ceremony and reception were over. I waited in the candlelight chamber of King Rolfe, my rose-perfumed pussy as ready as it would ever be to take the cock of my new husband.

At the foot of the bed stood the King, the High Meister, and worst of all, Aiden—the official witnesses of my 'first mating.' After it was over, I would be legally married and bound for life to the Prince of Crasmere.

Why could I not be opening my legs for Aiden?

When we danced and I pressed myself close to him, I felt how hard he was for me, the outline of his stiff cock, pressing close to my damp, quivering pussy. The more we moved, holding each other close, the more I imagined being filled by him. I had to stop myself from reaching down and stroking the protruding bulge in his tight uniform.

I cared not that hundreds of eyes in the great hall watched us. I would gladly let them witness him ravage me in the way I had dreamt of every night for the past two weeks as I pleasured myself in the privacy of my cottage hideaway.

I was made for Aiden. And now, I was about to be legally bound to his brother.

Why had I not just run away when Creena explained the first-mating ceremony to me and then led me up the long flight of stairs to the King's chamber? I could have fled before she removed my wedding gown and instructed me to 'present my virginity' on the bed. She allowed me the small dignity of covering my shoulders with a mink stole, though it barely covered the pale flesh of my breasts.

The King and Zachron nodded their heads as they watched me adjust the small fur covering. Aiden would not look me in the eye. He seemed in pain participating in such a ceremony. I knew he was a slave to obligation, deathly loyal to his family and the traditions of Braeyork. No matter what he might be feeling about being here watching his brother take my virginity, Aiden would do his duty as Virum Optimum.

But what about me? Was I so weak of mind and spirit as to willingly partake in such a degrading ritual? Why had I not fled and taken my chances with the wolves, bears, and other predators of the forest?

I kept searching for Aiden's eyes, praying he might at least look at me when I most needed him. He must have sensed my desperation. He finally turned around slowly and hunched his broad shoulders together. Our eyes locked together. Despite the gross indecency of the situation, perhaps he would not forsake me and somehow help me endure this horrible ritual.

I spread my legs apart a little. Did he understand I belonged to him, no matter what happened tonight? I would always belong only to Aiden. I bit my lip and spread my legs wider. He had never before seen me naked, and now I was showing him the soft white powdered hair above my manicured pussy lips. As we stared into the window of each other's hearts, I began to tremble.

I knew he wanted me. I was his, and he needed to take me now. I squirmed like a bitch in heat, my legs completely spread open for his hungry eyes. The urge to touch the hood of my tiny erect bud and stroke my aroused clit was overwhelming. The delicate folds of my pussy lips quivered open for Aiden.

The odor of my sex filled the King's Chamber. Aiden leaned in closer. I ignored the King and Zachron, who stared open-mouthed. I fixed my eyes on Aiden and mouthed my plea to him.

Take me, Aiden. Fill me with your thick cock. Release your seed inside me, and then fill me again and again...

Shane entered the chamber, the clomping of his heavy footfalls breaking the spell. I pulled my legs together and reached for the fur stole to wrap around my naked chest.

I could make out the dim outline of Shane's form as a looming shadow against the flickering candlelights. Another few steps and he stood by the edge of the bed in his boots. He appeared drunk, grunting a greeting at me, ignoring the group of witnesses huddled at the foot of the bed.

"Ready?" he growled, unfastening the belt, holding up open his trews, and kicking off his boots.

I was too frightened to reply. I knew I had to open my legs to him and receive the cock of my husband for the first time. I had one purpose—to offer him my virginity.

"I…" I could not speak the words. I glanced at Aiden. He shook his head slowly and looked up.

No! Please, I begged silently. Do not forsake me!

"She is more than ready," Zachron growled. "Your wife's cunt is wet with desire. She has even teased us with a lust rare for one so… inexperienced. She begs to be fucked for the first time. Fill her with royal seed, your Grace."

I pushed myself back higher in the bed, toward the pillows stacked against the headboard. I cowered, suddenly afraid to accept my bridal duty and offer myself to anyone other than Aiden.

Shane stood naked. He climbed onto the bed, his face and body wet with perspiration. His face seemed contorted, his eyes narrowing as I watched him crawl toward me on his hands and knees. His appearance seemed to be changing. Was it only my dread at what was about to happen?

Or was I really seeing scales transforming his skin into that of a reptile?

He hissed at me. A long, forked tongue protruded from his mouth. He raised himself on his knees. His cock curled from his body, long, thin and snake-like.

"Give me your virgin cunt!"

I screamed. "No!"

He jumped and, in an instant, pinned me down on the bed. His long snake cock curled and sought out the opening of my pussy. He spoke in an unfamiliar tone – the voice of one possessed by evil.

"I will breed you. Breed you until you bring forth a Serpen King to rule Braeyork for a thousand years!"

"No!" I wailed, this time in an ear-splitting screech. As the head of the thin cock touched the lips of my pussy, there was a commotion. Someone pushed the monster away.

"Serpen! Get off of her!"

Aiden stood, sword in hand, by the bed. Shane, or the creature he had become, turned and curled his body, hissing at Aiden. I watched in horror as the half-man, half-snake monster stiffened, ready to pounce.

11

AIDEN

My brother's face was now fully that of a serpen. I clutched my sword, sizing up the creature. It coiled, on the bed, its snake head swaying back and forth.

I raised my sword in the air. "What have you done with Shane?"

The creature hissed, head still moving from side to side. I followed its movements with my long sword raised high above my head.

"Shane is gone. The virgin is mine now." The voice of the creature was neither that of a man nor a woman. The hideous body, though, still carried something of Shane's visage; his face had merged with that of a snake.

And though it had no legs, a long thin cock protruded from the body, and its torso was still more man than serpen.

"Run, Elva!" I commanded as I rushed toward the creature.

But the man-serpen was too quick. It managed to evade my sword and bring its long tail around, slapping my father in the head and knocking him over.

Elva pressed herself back against the headboard as the creature wrapped its tail around my father's head.

"Once the King is gone, I will rule Braeyork using Shane's likeness. And after I breed the virgin, my heirs will rule for centuries!"

Zachron cowered in the corner, trying to stay hidden. The creature tightened its grip around my father.

The King's eyes bulged. He was being choked to death. Sputtering, he gasped, "Help me!"

The head of the serpen raised above me. All vestiges of its human form were gone, other than a hideous curved cock. It held my father in a chokehold with its tail.

I raised up my heavy sword, the Saxum steel blade razor sharp. But if I struck down the serpen, would I be killing my brother?

"Help!" my father croaked.

I lowered my eyes and drew a deep breath. And then, with one mighty swing, gripping the hilt of the sword with both hands, I swung at the creature and cut it deeply.

The grip of its tail around my father released, and then, in a flash, its tail wrapped around my leg. It pushed me to the ground. But I had wounded the creature. A greenish ooze dripped from its mouth. I was on my back, trying to reach for my fallen sword.

SOLD TO THE KING

It was too far away from me.

I could hear my father gasping for breath. The creature had wound its tail around my neck. I struggled to loosen its choking grip. I had always had a deathly fear of snakes, and now I was about to lose my life to one.

"Let him go!" A voice yelled out.

I turned toward the sound. Elva, still naked, held my heavy sword above her head.

The creature hissed at her. She stood defiant on the bed like a fierce warrior, though she struggled with the weight of the sword.

"It is me you want," she yelled, raising the sword with her trembling arms. "Let him go, and I am yours."

The serpen's tail around my neck loosened.

"Yesssss," it hissed. I could see the creature's thin cock stiffen. "You will take all of me inside your virgin hole."

Elva dropped the sword to the floor. I scrambled to my feet, and with one quick motion, she kicked the sword toward me.

"Fuck me now!" Elva moaned and threw herself on the bed, raising her ass up as if she wanted to be mounted.

The creature hissed again and turned toward her, its long cock ready to penetrate her. With a single motion, I scooped up the sword and then, with two hands, tightly gripped the hilt.

The serpen's head was raised up above Elva as it prepared to defile her. I lifted my sword, but the creature was too close to Elva.

Suddenly the voice of my father yelled out. "Stop!"

The serpen turned at the sound. My arms became one with the sword. I swung the blade and landed a deep blow to the neck of the creature. The steel blade struck flesh and bone with a sickening thud.

It hissed in pain. But it was not dead. A greenish-black liquid oozed from its wound, and it managed to curl its body once again and pounce on my father standing at the foot of the bed. Even so badly wounded, it was a powerful creature and managed to get a tight chokehold on the King.

"You can't kill me," the serpen hissed, its bloodied head glaring back at me. My father was being choked again, his eyes bulging as his face reddened. "I will snuff out the King and come back for the virgin when I'm–"

I swung the razor-sharp edge of my sword with every fibre of my strength at the gaping wound of the serpen. My aim was sure this time as I screamed in fury and sliced off the head of the snake.

The severed head fell to the stone floor. The rest of the body shrunk and dropped in a heap beside it on the floor.

SOLD TO THE KING

No one spoke as we all stood winded in the candlelit chamber.

Elva rushed to me, still naked. I removed my tailcoat and wrapped it around her. We held each other for a moment, both of us trembling.

"Look!" my father cried.

I released Elva and watched as the skin of the serpen began to move. It convulsed, shedding a layer of white scales, and to our amazement, a body seemed to be growing within it.

Zachron leaned over and tore away the dead skin. The face of Shane and the rest of his body emerged. He was unclothed and curled up as if a newborn child. He began to weep.

And then the molted skin he had shed beside him began to transform into a tiny snake. It slithered away and disappeared under the door.

"Shane?" My father bent down and touched the bare shoulder of my brother, who was still weeping on the floor. "Are you–"

"Leave me alone!" Shane cried. He seemed broken and tortured. "Let me out of here…"

Before anyone could say more, he ran from the chamber out the door.

Elva clung to me. I held her tightly.

Zachron whispered something in my father's ear. He nodded as he listened and then turned to me.

"You saved me, Aiden," my father said in a humble voice. "This night, you preserved the Crown of Braeyork from evil. I should have listened to you about the Serpen Queen."

I nodded, my arm still wrapped around Elva.

"The High Meister suggests, and I concur, that you should be rewarded with any title that I as the King, can bestow upon you."

"There is only one thing I desire, Father," I replied. "If she will have me, I want the hand of Elva as my wife."

She touched my cheek. "It is all I want as well."

"Then you shall take her as your first-wife," Zachron interjected with a toothy smile.

"I do not want her as a *first-wife*," I replied. "I want Elva as my *only* wife."

"No!" Zachron snapped, turning to my father. "As a Prince, second in line to the throne, a noble of the highest standing, he must uphold the rights of the nobility and take a second-wife and a –"

"I will not take a second-wife and I will not take a third-wife," I said firmly. "And I certainly will not make use of my father's harem. Elva is all I will ever need and ever desire."

My father looked uncomfortable at my tirade.

Zachron shook his head. "Your Grace, what he proposes will cause the Lords of the Dominion great concern. This is a direct threat to their privileges. They will withdraw support for the Crown, withhold tithes and renounce your name, unless…"

The High Meister hesitated.

"Unless what, Zachron?" My father asked impatiently.

"If Prince Aiden renounces his royal titles, the deeds of land drawn in his name, his inheritance and place in line to the throne and lives as a commoner away from Braeyork Castle, then–"

"I accept," I interjected.

My father did not look convinced. I could see he was torn by the proposal and by my hasty acceptance. "I owe you, Aiden. But before I allow you to do this, I must ask Elva."

He took a step toward her. "Are you willing to be the bride of a commoner, a man without rank or title?"

"I am," she replied quickly, "with all my heart."

"Then you must leave Braeyork Castle." My father stated simply. "I will offer you a single bar of Alum gold as your wedding gift."

"Thank you, Father." I smiled and glanced at Elva. And as we held each other's eyes, I remembered I still carried the wedding band in my pocket.

"Can you grant me one last request before we leave?" I asked, turning to his Majesty.

"If it is within my power, of course."

"Marry us. Here and now."

Zachron guffawed at the request. "That would be quite unorthodox. I can't–"

"Not you," I interrupted. "Father, as the King of the Braeyork Dominion, your word is law. Marry us here and give us your blessing."

I knew I was asking a lot of my Father. He touched his chin. "Do you still have the marriage band?"

"I do," I replied, pulling it from my pocket and handing it to him.

He studied it a moment. "Elva place your hand over the heart of Aiden."

She stepped forward, still wearing only my dark coat. She placed her hand on my chest.

"Do you, Elva, take this man as your husband, for now, and until death do you part?"

"I do."

My father handed me the ring. "Aiden, if you will take this woman as your wife, as long as you both shall live, place this band of gold on her finger as a symbol of your everlasting love and commitment and repeat after me, 'I thee wed.'"

Elva dropped her hand from my chest. I slid the ring onto her delicate finger.

"I thee wed," I said quietly.

And then we kissed for the first time as husband and wife.

12

ELVA

I wasn't sure what to expect as Aiden carried me through the door of the little cottage I had called home for the last two weeks. I wore my wedding dress and nothing underneath—as had been required for my first mating with Shane.

But unlike that disgusting ritual, no witnesses would watch as I accepted my husband for the first time.

Aiden set me down as we crossed the threshold of the small cottage. He closed the door and held me in the light of a glowing harvest moon glowing through the window. He held my hands to his lips.

"Wife," he whispered, kissing them gently, then touching my ring. "Wife," he repeated. "Can I say it over and over and over?"

The softness of his lips thrilled me. "Yes, husband. I very much like it. Say it again."

"Wife," his voice grew husky. He took my chin and raised it up close to his face. His lips grazed mine. "My wife. My love. Forever."

His lips crushed mine as I opened my mouth to him. He probed and explored me, and then I did the same to him. His grip around my back was firm.

Our bodies pressed together. Through my thin wedding gown, I could feel him growing hard, pressing between my legs. My pussy ached for his touch. But more than that, it longed for that cock growing so impossibly large between his legs.

We kept kissing even as we ground our bodies together against each other. The damp odor of my arousal filled the room. The deep kissing alone felt like it was going to make me explode.

Aiden pulled back and released me. "Elva, you are the most beautiful woman, the bravest soul and the most loving, desirable creature I have ever had the fortune to know."

I trembled at his words but also at the sight of him standing there before me. My *husband*. I was married now—to his dark, inviting eyes, to his long black hair and beard, the bulging muscles of his chest and, beneath that rich blue uniform, and to his thick, hard cock.

The cock that was about to make me a woman.

"I am afraid to close my eyes in case this is all but a dream," I whispered. The passion of our kiss had made me damp. I needed him to fill me up, to finally and gloriously claim what was his.

SOLD TO THE KING

And only his.

"It is not a dream. When the sun rises in the morning, we will start our first day together as man and wife," he smiled. "But my most precious Elva. I'm going to love you the way I've always dreamed, and I hope that you have too."

"I have," My face flushed. I needed his cock. I needed to finally ride it, to fuck my husband all night long, "I have dreamed of you every night."

"I'll light the fire," Aiden said.

I wasn't sure I could wait that long.

I watched him in a trance of desire, his strong hands breaking apart the kindling, then leaning over and softly blowing the tiny blue flame after striking the flint rock until the flames licked the dry wood he had carefully arranged. Within minutes a roaring fire crackled in the hearth. The dancing light brightened our cozy wedding night chamber.

He wiped his hand clean and led me to the edge of the bed. "Let me undress you, Elva."

"Yes. Please."

I was naked underneath my wedding gown.

He stared into my eyes as he lowered the straps around my shoulder. The firm globes of my breasts held the gown in place. He slowly peeled back the material covering them. His eyes widened at his first view of my naked bosom.

"Elva, you are even more perfect than I dreamed," he whispered, cupping my breasts with his palm, his thick fingers gently caressing the soft flesh before circling my excited nipples.

I moaned at his touch. He continued to squeeze me with one hand and, with the other, pushed my wedding gown down over my flat stomach, his hand lingering just about my damp pussy. He leaned forward and kissed me again, his tongue thrusting as if it was his cock he wanted me to taste.

I was melting from his caresses. He continued to massage my breasts as he pushed my dress all the way down with his other hand and cupped me between my legs, touching my womanhood for the first time.

I ground my thigh into him. He traced the outline of my pussy lips, wetting his finger with my moist excitement, and then slid up, teasing the underside of my tiny tingling bud. My clit begged for his attention.

"You are wet, wife," he spoke as he pulled his lips back from mine. His finger kept circling my clit and then dipping into my soaking wetness, teasing the opening of my pussy, before returning to my excited bud. I bucked my hips, aching for more.

"You are going to make me cum," I moaned.

He removed his hand and pushed me down on the bed. He flung away my bunched wedding gown, gathered around my feet, and spread my legs apart. I could see the fire in his eyes, an animal lust to mate me.

Aiden stepped back, and in the glow of the crackling fire, I watched him undo the buttons of his tunic. He opened it and threw it off. I drank in the sight of his rippled muscular chest. He began to unfasten his belt.

My pussy quivered at the anticipation of finally feasting my eyes on that cock, the one my ladies-in-waiting giggled and gossiped about – the thick, hard cock of my husband.

"Is it true that our marriage is not legal until…" I hesitated, "you mate me for the time?"

He nodded. "It is true. And I am about to make our marriage very, *very* legal."

"May I?" I needed to wrap my hands around his manhood, "touch it?"

He pulled me up from the bed. I leaned over, my big tits squeezing together as I finished undoing his belt and pulling down his trews.

His erect cock was bigger and harder than I had dreamt about all these past nights. I touched the head, bulging and swollen. The tip was wet with a drop of his cum. I smeared it over the purple head and then ran my hand down the thickly veined length of my husband's long shaft.

"Ohhhhhhh," he moaned, flinching at my touch. "I need you, Elva. I need to fuck you now."

"I need to be fucked."

He pushed me down on the bed and gathered me up under my shoulders, arranging me high on the bed. He pulled my legs apart and moved on top of me, his solid thighs pushing me further apart to accommodate his full girth. The head of his pulsing cock lightly grazed the wet opening of my gaping pussy hole.

He loomed over me, holding his cock with one hand as he began to caress my cunt with it. The head of him circling my entrance moving up to grind against my swollen clit.

Only when I was thrusting my hips up, eager for more, did he line the head of his cock with my wanton pussy. Slowly, he inched himself forward. Just the tip entered me, giving me the feeling of being deliciously full. But, he removed it again, still guiding his cock with one hand, pushing in the thick swollen head of his cock only to remove it once again.

Finally, out of sheer desperation, I reached for him, fingers biting into the firm globes of his ass and trying to drag him closer. I needed him, all of him.

"Take me," I moaned. "Take your wife."

With a rumbling guttural grunt, he pushed deep inside my virgin cunt.

I cried out with the sharp pain that shot through me as he broke my cherry. His cock thrust all the way to the very core of my womanhood. As the pain coursed through me, I stared at his face. His eyes were wet.

He touched my lips with a finger. I licked it, and he began to move his hips, pulling his cock out a bit and then slowly thrusting back inside me, deeper and sure, impaling me into the bed.

He stretched me open as he began to ride me. I rose to meet his thrusts, and soon we bucked together, both frantic to unite our loins, moving in perfect unison.

And then, as I felt him stiffen. My body began to convulse. I was cumming all over his thick cock. It spasmed and twitched as he screamed out and released his seed inside of me. He kept thrusting and thrusting until he was completely spent, and my pussy filled with my husband's cum for the first time.

13

AIDEN

I had never experienced anything like the feeling of releasing my seed inside of Elva.

My wife.

Yes, I had fucked other women, mostly the King's fuck dolls and one other who had offered herself to me to provide what her husband could not.

But being inside of Elva, my cock still pulsing from our first coupling as husband and wife, was what I had been born to do. To not only love and cherish her but also to pleasure her, make her scream and cum until she fell asleep with a deeply satisfied smile as she lay contentedly spent beneath me.

My cock remained hard inside her. I felt wetness oozing from her pussy, running down between us. I had opened her, and she baptized me with the crimson blood of her virginity.

I kissed her lightly and raised myself up a little. Her face glistened with perspiration, and her eyes were wet with tears.

"Now we are married," I whispered. "Legally bound forever, an unbreakable bond."

"I am yours," Elva's voice seemed like an angel's whisper. "I am full of your seed."

I gently outlined her face with a finger, touching her nose and her chin, grazing her lips, and gently brushing her cheeks.

"Your face is more perfect even than what I imagined every night as I closed my eyes." I smiled. "And now it will be the last thing I see every night as I fall asleep."

She raised a hand to my cheek. "After you love me like this?" Her hips tightened, squeezing my cock.

I laughed. "Yes, every night. Every single night... if that is your desire."

In response, her hands wrapped around the top of my shoulders, lightly massaging them. Her hips pushed against mine. "I will always want you. Will you fuck me this good every night?"

My cock stiffened even more at her frank request. I raised my body up, feasting on her naked tits. I played with her nipples, gently pinching and then licking them before I began to grind into her slowly.

"Is this what you need, wife? My cock inside you... fucking you... mating you?"

"Yesssssss!" she moaned as I pulled the full length of my long cock out of her soaking pussy but kept the fat head plugging her wet entrance. "Fuck me all night..."

She bucked her hips up, moaning. "Mate me, husband!"

I pushed back into her, feeling her tight, narrow cunt walls squeezing my cock, urging me to possess her like an animal in heat. My cock throbbed with the thrill of filling her so completely.

We moved together as one, and then, still inside her pussy, I rolled her over in one quick motion, and she was on top of me.

I grabbed her round ass as I rose up to thrust inside her. Her big, firm tits bounced up and down as we fucked. She leaned over and fed me one of her pale white tits. I sucked the erect brown nipple in my mouth, feasting on her until she moved and fed me her other breast.

And then she pulled away, raising her head up, lost in the pleasure as she rode my cock.

"Mmmmmmm," she groaned as she slowly raised herself up high and then slowly dropped down until I was deeper inside of her than I thought possible.

She was grinding now, milking my cock. I thrust up slowly and began to feel cum rising from my balls.

"Ohhhhhh…" We both moaned together.

As I felt the urge to cum strengthen, I flipped her over again and pinned Elva down on the bed. I needed release again inside my wife. I pinned her down on the bed with my body, holding both her wrists above her head, leaving Elva open to my greedy eyes.

"Take me!" she rasped.

I pushed into her like a crazed beast. She met every thrust with a deep groan of lust. We thrashed together in a wild frenzy as the cum in my cock rose high and higher.

And then we both screamed as I spasmed and I began to spurt my load. Her fingers dug into my back, clawing like an impaled beast. As cum shot out of me, her piercing shrieks echoed through the cottage.

My cock emptied inside her once more on our wedding night as her cries turned to soft whimpers. We collapsed exhausted into each's arms and soon drifted into a satiated sleep in the glow of the dying fire.

We slept naked in our spent stupor. When the first light of dawn brightened the room, I felt Elva stirring, still wrapped in my arms.

Her smiling face was the last thing I remember seeing before falling asleep and the first thing that greeted my eyes as I blinked them open.

"Was it all real?" Her emerald eyes had a faraway look.

"Yes, my love," I whispered, touching her cheek. "We are husband and wife."

She grinned, closed her eyes a moment, and then, opening them, stared at me and purred. That is how I would describe the sound she released, like that of a contented creature whose every need had been met.

We lay together in each other's arms, enjoying the sensation of our naked bodies next to each other. I stroked her long, flaxen hair and massaged her back while she caressed my neck with her soft hands. Her gentle cooing was our only conversation, and before long, we drifted back to sleep again, locked in our embrace.

After we awoke a few hours later, cleaned ourselves, made tea, and warmed bread and cakes, we sat down in the afterglow of our wedding night.

Elva wore a simple peasant blouse but no skirt. I wore only the pants of my uniform, as she insisted I remain barechested 'forever.' I laughed but was proud she found my body pleasing.

After we had our fill of breakfast, she moved her chair closer and stroked my chest, teasing my nipples, squeezing my bulging biceps, and paying special attention to my hard stomach.

"Is it true what you said last night?" she asked with a tease in her voice. "Did you mean what you told the King, that you would not take a second or a third-wife, and…" she dropped her hand lower over my pants, "you will not make use of the King's fuck dolls?"

The feeling of her fingers on my pants, squeezing the outline of my cock, excited me. I squirmed in the seat. I strained in the confines of my tight pants as she traced my organ with her fingers.

"Yes," I groaned. "You are all I will ever need."

Elva stopped teasing me and touched my mouth with her finger. "But if I am to please you, husband, you must help me understand. What does a second-wife, and a third-wife provide that a first-wife does not."

I pulled my legs together. Her touch had hardened me. I tried to adjust myself to relieve the pressure. "You must not worry about that, Elva. You thrill me completely. Even looking at you excites me more than any–"

"Tell me," she pouted playfully. "Or I won't let you touch me." She grinned, "ever again."

I chuckled. "Well, then, you leave me no choice." I folded my hands, looking up to find the words to explain. "A first-wife is treasured, revered, as if upon a pedestal. She is the Queen of a noble's home, and if you had married Shane—you would have become the Queen of Braeyork. A first-wife must be proper and docile. She takes her husband's seed so she may bear him children. Her role is to become a mother and supervise the children's upbringing."

Elva shook her head. "And in bed, with her husband…" she hesitated.

"She is a lady." I smiled. "She takes him inside her and kisses him goodnight."

"I see," Elva frowned. "So… then, when a husband visits his *second-wife,* what does *she* do?"

I could see she wanted details, and I was loathed to say more.

"I want to know. Tell me, please! Tell me the same way you would explain to a man."

I shook my head again. "Okay, if you must know, a second-wife takes her husband whenever he feels the urge—inside her pussy, in her mouth, or if he desires, she might stroke him until he cums all over her."

I was shocked at myself for being so frank, but she wanted details. "And she does not carry his child?"

"No. The High Meister gives her a potion of milk of penny-royal and tansy, to make sure her husband's seed will not grow within her."

Elva nodded. She placed her hands again over my trousers, rubbing slowly. I twitched as she found the head of my cock. "And what comforts does a *third-wife* provide?"

It was hard to answer her question while her hands continued to stroke me. "Well, she, is like a second-wife, but she will go even further to pleasure her husband." I hesitated. "Sometimes… much, much further."

Elva took two fingers and ran them down my pants, tracing the outline of my cock. "Further? How?"

I moaned. "You're making me hard."

She stopped stroking. "Good. Now tell me what a third-wife does." She began to unbuckle my belt.

I exhaled at the site of my wife, the cleavage of her heaving tits trapped in her low-cut peasant blouse. She slid her hand inside my pants.

"Tell me, husband," she cooed as her hand fished deeper until she wrapped her fingers around the shaft of my cock, "tell me, or I'll stop."

"She offers her asshole," I moaned. "She fucks him in front of other men. She strips for him, and if he desires, she will take two cocks at the same time. Or, she will bring a fuck doll to join them in their bedroom. Whatever he needs… a third-wife provides without hesitation."

Elva pulled my cock out of my pants and stroked me slowly. "And what do you need, husband?"

I lifted her blouse and pulled her to me as she straddled my lap. I kissed her deeply and massaged her tits. And then, without another word, she dropped to her knees and began to stroke my excited cock.

"Let me be *all* your wives, Aiden."

As she stroked, her voice lowered, and she touched the tip of her tongue to my cock.

"I want to taste your cum. I want to feel you in every hole. I want to excite you—the way you excite me."

"Oh fuck," I moaned as I fed my cock into her hungry mouth. It was a soft fuck hole, and though she could barely get even the head of my cock in her mouth, she eagerly opened wider and wider until she gagged on my throbbing organ.

I held her head and fucked her mouth. Her tits bounced up and down as I used her mouth. After a moment, she slowed, and I pulled out. Her saliva dripped from my cock.

"Let me be your fuck doll, husband. I need your cum all over me."

She opened her mouth, and I pushed it back in and pumped. Her tongue teased the head, and I could feel my control weakening as she used her hand to stroke the shaft of my cock that did not fit into her mouth, gently cupping my balls with her other hand.

I shuddered but held her head on my cock as I began to spurt my load into her mouth until it overflowed.

She took some of my cum and dabbed it over her nipples and onto her face. It was as if I had marked her against any other man.

"You are all I will ever need," I said, trying to get my breath. "Now, let me taste your pussy and make you cum until you scream. And then I will make you cum again and again and again."

14

ELVA

The journey to the Passview Western Territories was a long and arduous journey. I cared not that we rode ten hours most days—Aiden on his black mare, me holding the reins of the horse pulling our covered wagon. I blossomed in the love of my husband, and my legs bowed most mornings from a night that started with slow, gentle lovemaking and ended with screams of thrashing delight.

My body was truly alive for the first time in my life. I had never before known what it meant to be pleasured and to pleasure, to love completely and to be loved completely in return. As I stroked Aiden's chest every night after we lay spent in each other's embrace, we talked of our dreams for the future, about names for our children, and of growing old together.

After almost three weeks of dusty trails, a few long misty, rainy days, and after passing through dozens of tiny villages, we finally arrived at the outermost shire—Goldenleaf.

Beyond its borders lay the vast and wild Passview Western Territories. We stopped briefly to water our horses and take on supplies. A wizened old man warned Aiden about going further west.

"Your Father's kingdom ends here," the man told Aiden. "King Rolfe may claim the western territories as his own, but he has no soldiers to enforce his rule."

I watched Aiden listen carefully to every word the old man spoke. My husband did not seem concerned. "They speak our language," he said simply. "That is good enough for me."

The man spat on the ground. "You can't trust anyone in the Passview. They respect no one."

"Well then," Aiden grinned, glancing over at me. "I like them already."

With that, he mounted his horse, and I climbed up onto the wagon. With a crack of our reins, we proceeded west, following the trail leading out of Goldenleaf and within thirty minutes, came to a stone archway. In the distance, I could see wide open fields of long golden grass bending under the afternoon sun. Far off in the distance, imposing mountain peaks touched the clouds.

After we crossed through the archway, Aiden turned Champian around and rode next to me as we took our first few steps into the Passview Western Territory.

"We are free now, my love," Aiden called out. "Free to be who we are and who we were meant to be."

I nodded. Something about the expanse of open grasslands, with cattle and sheep grazing in the distance and the snow-capped mountains rising through the haze, filled me with the promise of unlimited possibilities.

"Yes. We are home, husband."

We spent our first two nights in the Passview Territories sleeping in our wagon beneath a brilliant sky of shooting stars and the faint outline of a new moon. Somehow, we were even more in love than before. Maybe it was the open spaces of this place, the feeling that anything and everything was possible here.

I spread my legs wide to Aiden in the warmth of our cozy wagon. He raised up my blouse and teased my erect nipples. My breasts were even more full than usual, and I sensed new life might soon be growing within me. His tongue played a long time on my nipples until I was moaning and feeling dampness overtaking my pussy.

I needed Aiden so badly it hurt. I stroked his long hair as he feasted on my tits. "You're going to make me cum," I moaned, squirming and undulating.

"Good," he replied without slowing. His hand wandered down between my legs and touched the swollen lips of my pussy. He teased the opening of my cunt. "You are wet, wife."

I couldn't take it and felt myself beginning to lose control. He fucked me with his fingers as he kept sucking my tits, and soon, I was bucking like an untamed mare. He slid down my stomach until his tongue found my erect clit. He circled it slowly, even as his fingers kept sliding in and out of my pussy lips.

"Oh fuck," I moaned as his tongue finally covered my clit, and he pushed two of his thick fingers inside of me. I began to feel my climax, raising my hips against his face and beard. He kept licking me and fucking me with his fingers until I began to squirt cum juice all over his face.

He released his hold on my legs and raised himself up, sliding on top of me until his lips found mine. I tasted myself on his tongue and felt my wetness on his beard. I needed his cock inside me, and without another word, he pushed into my soaking cunt.

Delirious with the pleasure he was bringing me, I felt my passion beginning to rise once more. Could I really cum again so quickly? He pushed in deeper, impaling me like he owned every inch of my body.

I was his completely. Not just his wife, I was his whore. "Aiden, use me," I whispered. "I am yours... in every way."

My words seemed to make his cock grow even harder.

"Let me be your fuck doll." I moaned. "Take my ass, please!"

Aiden thrust into me as his mouth covered mine. His cock was going deeper and feeling bigger than I had ever felt. Could I take it all in my asshole?

"Are you sure?" He pushed himself up on the bed.

His cock slipped out of me, and suddenly, I was empty. I needed to be filled.

"I want to be your whore," I said in a dark voice. I turned over on the bed and gathered my knees under me. I stuck my round virgin ass up in the air, waiting to be mounted.

"Take me!" I groaned, pushing my face into the soft furs of our bed.

I knelt anxiously as a wet finger touched my virgin asshole. Slowly Aiden opened me and began to prepare me for something much bigger.

"My wife, my fuck doll, my virgin whore," he whispered as he removed his finger, and I felt the head of his slippery cock pushing against my ass, sliding around and then, ever so slowly, opening me.

Aiden's thick fingers gripped my ass cheeks tightly as he began to inch his way inside me. The pain at first made me gag, but as more and more of his cock entered, the union of pain and pleasure overwhelmed me.

"Take me," Aiden whispered, holding my ass like he owned me.

I groaned. "Give me your seed. Use your whore."

Aiden began to pump. His hand reached under and found my clit as he fucked my ass. The feeling was unlike anything I had ever experienced. With a few strokes of his fingers on my swollen clit I began to cum.

Aiden thrust in deeper. "I want your ass!"

We both screamed as his cock spasmed. My body shook with an explosion of pleasure to the moaning cries of my husband. He held my ass cheeks as he screamed out, trembling with one final thrust as he emptied his seed deep inside me.

He held me still a moment before he pulled out, and we fell together on the bed.

We were a single entity, a thing unable to live without the other.

Complete and fulfilled.

Forever.

The next morning, we had our first contact with the people of the Passview Western Territories. Word had gotten around that Aiden was the son of King Rolfe. A small group of men arrived on horseback at our camp as we were finishing up a breakfast of tea, bread, and cheese.

"Is it true?" an older man who appeared to be the leader of the group asked as he approached us. "You are Prince Aiden, sent by your father, the King, to take charge of Passview?"

Aiden extended a hand to the man. "I'm Aiden, no longer a Prince, sir. I'm a man like you. Nothing more."

The man, dressed in casual but colorful clothing, shook Aiden's hand. "I am Bolivar. Bolivar Doone. Why are you here then?"

My husband didn't respond immediately. He seemed to be sizing up Bolivar and glancing at his two younger and possibly related companions based on their similar looks. "I have not come on behalf of my Father, and I certainly did not come to take charge of Passview."

Aiden turned toward me and waved me over. "This is my wife, Elva."

I stood up, shuffled over, and stood beside Aiden. All eyes turned toward me, and the two younger men blushed and looked away.

"We are seeking a new life, away from the customs of Braeyork, many of which we do not condone," Aiden explained to Bolivar and his companions. "We wish to raise our family here."

Bolivar nodded. "You know nothing of our ways and our land or of our people. Most strangers do not stay long."

My husband glanced at me as if looking for my approval to make this our home. I nodded. He bent down and kissed my forehead. Without another word, he walked over to our covered wagon, reached inside the flaps, and undid the straps of a leather satchel bolted to the floorboards.

He returned and stood before Bolivar. "This is a bar of pure Alum gold," he announced, extracting our wedding gift from the King. "I want to buy land here, build a house and hire men to help harvest what gifts this land may provide."

Aiden handed the gold bar to Bolivar. He examined it carefully and gave his companions an opportunity to hold it as well. They murmured to each other in a tongue I did not understand.

Bolivar handed the gold bar back to Aiden.

"With this much gold, you could have a life of ease here and never work another day for the rest of your life," Bolivar said with a skeptical tone.

"No. My wife and I wish to work, to build something here of our own. And someday, I will repay my father for his gift and teach my sons and daughters to follow their dreams wherever they lead."

I studied Bolivar's face for signs of his reaction to Aiden's pronouncements. The man was deeply tanned, his hair just beginning to show streaks of gray. He held his jaw clenched, and I could not tell what effect my husband's words had made upon him.

But then Bolivar's face softened. He smiled as he reached out his hand to Aiden.

"Welcome to Passview!"

15

AIDEN

The first two months in the Passview territories were filled with more hard work and setbacks than I had experienced in all of my twenty-six years. Most days brought back-breaking labor setting up the farm I purchased and frustrating delays in finalizing my acquisition of the old shipyards I planned to renovate.

My goal was to start building a new generation of square-rigged four-mast sailing ships.

I had even found a master builder, Douglas, who inspired me with his theory of using iron on the vessels to reinforce the hulls and to place masts for and aft for additional speed. The new ships would help not only the people of the Passview, but all of the Braeyork Dominion to become a true trading empire.

But the wheels of commerce turned slowly in the Passview Western territories, even for a man with means. Most days when I was not working our farm, I spent embroiled in the details of deeds, letters, and negotiations with the current owners of the old dilapidated shipyards that dominated Passview harbor.

At home, though, the nights were filled with the pleasure of loving Elva. We still awaited the joy of knowing that a new life had taken hold in her womb. Even though she had not yet missed any of her monthly courses, we believed it was only a matter of time.

Every night, tired as I might be, I found comfort inside her welcoming pussy or warm mouth. Some nights she liked to tease and arouse me until I couldn't help but fuck her hard and deep. She loved my tongue, and I happily complied with her wishes.

I loved sucking her clit and tongue fucking her until screams of pleasure rang through our simple farmhouse, and her love juice washed over my bearded face.

Today, however, I knew something was amiss the moment I approached the farmhouse. I'd spent the day repairing fences along the southern ridge of our rolling sheep pasture. I was surprised to see Bolivar Doone hitch the reins of his black mare to a post near the horse barn.

"Bolivar," I called out as I lugged my heavy sack of tools and set them on a bench beside the barn. "It's good to see you again."

Bolivar acknowledged me with a nod but not a smile. "Have you got a moment, Prince Aiden?"

Despite the many times I told Bolivar to call me 'Aiden,' he occasionally used my formal title when introducing me to men of commerce or those who held formal titles in Passview.

I shook his hand. "Of course. Will you come inside?"

"Yes. Your wife should hear the news too."

"Well, come in then. Let me offer you something to drink."

He sighed and followed me through the front entrance to our house. As I walked in, Elva was about to embarrass herself with her usual groping of me when I gently pushed her away.

"Bolivar is here," I whispered, "with news."

Her bubbly smile faded. "News?"

I shrugged my shoulders as I gathered glasses and a bottle of the dark crimson Passview liquor, *Feenum.* I poured shots for all three of us and set them on the table.

Bolivar downed his in a single gulp. "Thank you."

Elva sat at the table, holding her glass. "Thank you, Bolivar, for your help finding such a healthy ram for our flock. We're hoping for many lambs in the spring." She grinned. "And our ewes seem much more content since he arrived."

"That's good news," he replied, holding his empty glass, studying it a moment before laying it down carefully on the wooden table. "But I'm afraid the news I bring is not so joyous."

I sat down at the table and reached for my glass of the crimson liquor. "Tell us, Bolivar. What is it?"

"The King is dead."

"What?" I gulped. "When?"

He waved for the bottle, and I poured him another shot. "Maybe a month ago? News travels slowly to the Passview." He downed his second shot and set the empty glass down carefully on the table.

"It must have been not long after you left Braeyork Castle." Bolivar clenched his lips together. "He died in his sleep, thankfully. Though we didn't know him well in the Passview, and some never accepted his authority, I believed King Rolfe a man of honor."

An image of my father teaching me to ride, helping me up to my first pony and laughing as I took to the reins flashed through my mind.

"Yes, he was a good man but not without faults," I replied, recalling our many disagreements. "But I loved him and believed he cared deeply about his subjects."

Bolivar held his mouth open. I sensed he had more news. "Your brother, Shane, has been crowned. He is now the King of Braeyork. And he..."

The hesitation worried me. "He... what?"

"He beheaded his stepmother, Lady Ursula, the day after his coronation."

"What?" Elva and I gasped at the same time.

"No, no!" she cried out. "What about the…"

"The King ordered her body burned at the stake." Bolivar spat on the floor. "She was with child. The new King claims she was bewitched and fornicated with women. He believed the child in her womb was fathered by the Serpen."

"No, no, no, no, no!" Elva broke down, weeping. "No, no… poor, poor, Ursula."

The knot in my stomach made it difficult to draw breath. "Is there any way to verify such… dark news?"

"Two different riders reported the same story. And a new arrival fleeing from the East, confirmed it as well. He also warned us that King Shane is demanding new tithes to build up his guards and that he is planning the biggest wedding in the history of Braeyork."

"Wedding?" I repeated.

"Yes, to the daughter of Philip of Hart, Lady Marion."

fter Bolivar left our home, I held Elva in my arms and let her weep. She trembled as I held her, unable to speak for a long time.

Many thoughts crossed my mind as I tried to console my wife. The image of the cruelties inflicted on poor Ursula was difficult to purge. I prayed she died quickly, and the baby in her womb felt no pain.

Still, the rage at Shane for acting in such an immoral manner enraged me. Should I return to Braeyork Castle and seek revenge and retribution in the name of Father and my stepmother? Did such a monster as Shane deserve to rule over the people of Braeyork?

"How could he do this?" Elva sobbed between gasping breaths.

Elva shared details about her afternoon with Ursula with me. I listened without judgment to the story of my lonely stepmother and how Elva had brought her a tiny modicum of happiness, a brief respite from her dreary isolation.

"I almost married Shane!" Elva shrieked at the realization of how close she came to being the wife of the new King.

"And now, Lady Marion will become his first-wife," I sighed. "Her father commands a legion of barded horses, and along with the nobles of Rochford, Shane and his father-in-law will be even more powerful than my father ever dreamed."

"And more ruthless," Elva added.

I thought of Lady Marion, sitting by the gardens of Hart Castle. She would no doubt accept her role as Shane's first-wife and turn a blind eye to his second and third wives and his harem of fuck dolls.

"How can she do it, Lady Marion?" Elva asked as she dried her tears. "Marry a man like that? Did you say she does not expect to be loved?"

"Yes, very sad. But she will undoubtedly make a perfect first-wife for my brother."

We talked long into the night until Elva finally drifted off to sleep with my arm around her and her head nestled into the

SOLD TO THE KING

crook of my shoulder. I closed my eyes, listening to her shallow breathing, lightly stroking her bare shoulder.

Much of the world was an evil place.

But no matter the odds, we would fight for love and decency all the days of our lives by caring not only for each other but also for all the good people of Braeyork.

EPILOGUE

FOUR YEARS LATER

As I watched young Aiden running behind his father, I couldn't help laughing at the way my son imitated everything he saw, especially the senior Aiden. Our little girl was only a few months old, and the two Aidens were now pretty much taking care of each other without me.

Well, most of the time, at least.

"Mama!" little Aiden called as he ran past his father. "Papa says I can build a fort!"

I smiled as Aiden scooped up the younger version of himself and tossed him in the air. This was their usual routine after coming in from the fields for our noon meal. After they cleaned themselves up, we sat around the table while I finished breastfeeding young Gracia.

The two Aidens gobbled up the lamb stew with chunks of the fresh bread I'd made this morning. After a few minutes, little Aiden was done and asked if he could go and play outside. As he ran away happily, I laid little Gracia in her bassinet and pulled my chair up beside my husband.

Our passion was still electric, even after two babies and four years of long, hard days. I teased his unruly hair, and he massaged my bare leg, running a hand up between my thighs under my loose dress.

"Mmmm," I purred, thinking about being alone with him tonight. "Don't stop."

His hand parted my legs, sneaking his fingers under my chemise. He teased my pussy lips until I moaned, but then pulled his hand away and touched my lips with a wet finger.

"Tonight, my love," he whispered. "I can't wait to taste you."

I was so worked up that I wasn't sure I could hold out that long. I would return the favor if he let me, taking his big cock in my mouth until he was ready to give me a good hard fucking. We'd missed a couple of nights out of sheer exhaustion, but tonight, we would make up for it.

Aiden took a swig of ale from his mug and stood. "We're going to finish it today, Elva. Can you believe it? The first four-mast ship to be built in Passview? And we have orders for three more!"

He leaned down to kiss me, and I pulled his head closer. I wanted to explore his mouth, and I pushed my tongue inside, showing how much I wanted him. He squeezed my breasts as we kissed but then pulled away.

"Tonight, Elva. I am going to fuck you so good."

And then he was gone, and I struggled to compose myself. Within a few minutes, little Aiden was ready for his nap, and Gracia was crying to be fed. I happily attended to them and thought about how far we'd come since arriving in Passview.

Our farm was prospering after Aiden hired men to manage the day-t0-day work while he set out to harvest the rich timber resources in the forests beyond the ridge. It was part of his plan to rebuild Passview's floundering shipyard. He spared no expense in developing a new generation of sailing vessels, the first of which would soon begin her maiden voyage at sea.

We were happy beyond anything I could have ever imagined. Even rumours of the Serpen Queen returning to Braeyork, and the occasional troubling story of King Shane's latest deed could not spoil what Aiden and I had built.

Our love was endless, and our passion boundless. I even smiled at the whispers of the Serpen Queen, for without her, I would be living in Braeyork Castle as the kept first-wife of a despicable King.

Instead, I was Aiden's queen.

And I would treasure that every day for the rest of my life.

The End

LEAVE A REVIEW!

If you enjoyed *Sold to the King, The Legends of Braeyork, Book 1,* please consider leaving an honest review.

Your opinion matters to other readers searching for stories like this one - erotic romance set in a world of historical fantasy.

You can leave a review on Amazon, Goodreads or BookBub.

Thank you so much for reading. I hope you enjoyed the story!

TAKEN BY THE MANBEAST

PREVIEW OF BOOK 2, LEGENDS OF
BRAEYORK

CHAPTER 1 - TAKEN BY THE MANBEAST

FLAME

I probably should have known that being the only woman in a pub overflowing with strong ale and even stronger intoxicated soldiers would lead to trouble. As the conversations grew increasingly raunchy and the supply of my grandfather's hearty Dunfeld ale began to dwindle, trouble certainly seemed about to spill over.

"You a maiden yet, wench? How old are you, girl?"

I dropped an overflowing tankard of dark ale on the table of the uniformed man posing the question. His drunk companions grunted, leering at me with a mouthful of filthy teeth.

I glared at the questioner. Captain Mason Hawke, the odorous commander of the King's cavalry, had arrived late last night. Beads of sweat covered my forehead. My thin blouse, drenched from the spray of pouring and serving hundreds of rounds of foaming beer, clung to me like a second skin. The soaked material barely hid the fullness of my breasts and my dark nipples from a room full of wanton eyes.

"None of your business, sir," I snorted.

I dared not show an ounce of weakness. If I let him know I had just turned twenty or lost my composure and revealed the secret of my true Fae nature, the morning would end even worse than the last two hours of being ogled and pawed by the rowdy mob of men in my grandfather's tiny establishment. The Painted Owl was the only inn and pub in the remote village of Dunfeld.

Despite my terse response, Captain Hawke smiled as he lifted his glass and drank deeply, draining half of the ale before setting it down, wiping his lips, and releasing a foul belch.

"You're Flame. Right?"

He inspected me up and down, nodding his head and licking his lips like a slobbering dog. "And are you a *natural* ginger?" he laughed, glancing at the other two dimwitted officers sitting with him.

One reached over and grabbed my arm.

"Ginger all over?" Captain Hawke sneered as the man tightened his grip around my wrist. "Maybe you should show us more, girl, so we don't have to be left wondering when we dream about you alone in our bunks tonight with only our hand to give us… *comfort.*"

The grinning officer was hurting me as he twisted my wrist, forcing my arm behind me.

"Leave her alone!"

The commanding tone of my grandfather Omar broke the officer's hold. Omar stepped closer, nodding for me to return to the bar. I took a step back, but the hand of Captain reached for my arm and held it firmly.

"Stay with me, Ginger," he laughed, rising to face my grandfather.

Both were imposing men. Only Omar's grey hair and beard hinted at a man of sixty. Captain Hawke belched again and curled his thin purple lips.

"She somethin' to you?" Hawke sneered. "My little Miss Ginger?"

"My granddaughter," Omar snarled. "Let her go. My ale's running low. It's time for you and your men to leave."

I glanced around the room, which had grown quiet. Unshaven and dishevelled soldiers watched the drama with leering grins. All that is, except for one tall groomed soldier, sitting alone at the far corner table. His penetrating eyes caught mine.

Don't worry. I'm here.

The words filled my mind as if someone was talking to me. The striking dark-eyed man in the corner nodded.

The Captain yanked my arm and scowled at my grandfather. "I'll leave when you pay the Crown Tithes and taxes we came here to collect. One gold coin for your inn and one hundred bushels of wheat for the Crown farmlands the King graciously allows you to till for him."

"Are you insane?" my grandfather retorted. "The Painted Owl barely makes a dozen copper pennies. And last year, we struggled to pay fifty bushels in rent."

The Captain locked his arm around my waist. "King Shane has doubled the Crown Tithes, sir. And all inns and pubs in Braeyork now pay a gold coin tax if they wish to sell their ale."

"I can't pay that!" Omar cried. "I have no gold coins. And a hundred bushels of wheat? We won't have enough left to live on. We'll starve."

Captain Hawke twisted my arm around and then yanked me to him. His breath stank of belched ale. He pressed his pocked face to mine. Without looking away, he grinned.

"I can reduce the rent if we can make a deal for Ginger here. The King's third-wife was beheaded last week for insubordination, and his stock of fuck dolls runs low."

"Never!" my grandfather shouted, trying to grab me away from Captain Hawke.

The two officers sitting at the table jumped up and restrained my grandfather, pushing him to the floor. One of them pressed his head to the floor under the sole of a heavy black boot.

"Nice view, Omar?" the Captain chuckled. "Why don't we make a deal?" He squeezed my chin and started to kiss me, trying to snake his thick tongue into my mouth. He groped one of my breasts, kneading the mass of it firmly in his hand while his tongue protruded into my throat.

I froze at the shock of his lewd action, made even sicker by his swine-like grunting.

I tried to free myself, but the Captain held his other hand around my stomach as he fondled my breast. He ground his loins into my backside while the men in the pub cheered him on.

Burning with rage, I imagined getting my hands around his neck. I wanted to hurt him like he was hurting me—choke the very life out of this disgusting pig.

I closed my eyes and clenched my teeth, imagining myself choking this animal to death.

CHAPTER 2 - TAKEN BY THE MANBEAST

THERON

How much more of this could I take without hating myself for watching? Watching and doing nothing to stop the filthy bastard.

Until now, I had managed to keep a low profile as a member of the Calvary, the King's elite Guard. I kept my emotions in check, fearful of the consequences of letting the beast within me take control should I give in to the constant rage as I reluctantly followed the orders of Captain Mason Hawke.

But watching him molest this young woman was the final straw.

Walking into the inn this morning with the rest of the men, I couldn't help but stare at her as if I had been struck by a thunderbolt from the gods.

Flame.

Her name suited her perfectly. The color of her long hair reminded me of a glowing sunset, casting waves of burning orange and fiery red as far as the eye could see.

Her mysterious olive-shaped eyes, when they caught mine just now, were impossibly curious and passionate – flecks of forest green surrounded by a pool of turquoise. But there was more, something mysterious and hidden about this woman. And try as I might, I could not help, but lust after the swell of her breasts and the curves of her wide hips revealed so clearly in her soaked clothing.

I knew every man in this crowded pub wanted exactly the same as me – to see her naked, to fuck, and ultimately possess her. But I feared I would end up hurting her. If the wolf blood of my father, a wild Midnight Lupus who had mated my mother, took control of my body, my man-beast cock would be more than she could handle.

But my intentions were not driven by lust. I had connected to her, hearing Flame's pleas in my mind as she struggled against the Captain's unwelcome molestation.

I need to choke him, kill this monster!

As I watched her struggle, anger overtook me. A primal urge to extinguish the source of her torment coursed through me. My uniform tightened around my chest and loins. Canine teeth lengthened in my mouth until I licked my lips and brushed back the snowy white hair covering my face.

I pounced from the table where I had been sitting, knocked over two men in front of me, and lept toward the front of the pub.

Hold on, Flame. I'm here!

If I could hear her thoughts, I hoped she might hear mine.

With a few powerful leaps, I rushed towards the Captain and knocked him off Flame. She tumbled to the floor. Our eyes locked together.

I won't hurt you.

She held her mouth, staring at me. In that fleeting moment, seeing her sprawled on her stomach with the top of her breasts spilling out of her damp blouse, I knew I would never be complete unless I mated her, filled her up with my man-beast cock, and marked her as mine.

Her eyes flickered. There was a look of terror on her face.

What are you?

Her trembling voice echoed in my mind. I hated that she feared me.

Before I could reply, the Captain punched me in the gut, and I howled in pain. But the raging Midnight Lupus deep inside me, the wolf blood of my father, had been aroused. I growled and threw myself on top of the Captain.

He tried to push me away. I grabbed and held him tightly, letting my sharp fangs pierce the soft meat of his left thigh. I tasted blood as he screamed in agony. Soldiers rushed towards us, swords raised.

"Kill the beast!" the Captain screamed as I twisted my head back and forth, my fangs embedded in his leg.

I could see swords held above my head. The soldiers hesitated, unable to strike me without lancing the Captain's leg. He tried to push me away.

"Get off me!"

I let him go and scrambled to my feet, snarling at the soldiers who circled me with their swords, ready to strike me down.

Captain Hawke managed to get up with the help of his two officers. "Bring me the wench!" he screamed, holding his leg where I'd bitten into him.

The officers scooped up Flame and held her in front of the Captain. Still holding the wound I'd inflicted on him with one hand, he reached under the poor girl's skirt with his other hand and cupped her between the legs.

"Leave her alone!" I snarled.

The Captain shot me a look of hate as he fondled Flame. "This belongs to me now. I'll take whatever I want."

"You monster!" I screamed, and as I was about to rush toward him, a thick arm wrapped around my neck tightly. A sword raised up over my head.

"Kill him!" the Captain shouted.

A sudden burst of terror filled me with a power I'd never experienced. I yanked the arm holding me by my neck and jumped out of the way of the falling sword.

I was badly outnumbered. I had to think quickly. Two men still held Flame as the Captain pressed his hand tightly between her legs.

I shot a glance at her.

I will kill him for what he's doing to you.

She stared at me with a look of confusion. I nodded before jumping at the two men holding Flame and knocking them over, pushing her and the Captain over as well.

In confusion, I lept over the soldiers standing in front of the wooden door of the pub. I rushed it, hoping I had enough strength to knock it down. I rammed the door with every ounce of power I could harness, jarring it loose from the hinges.

With one more powerful lunge, I knocked it over and fell onto the frozen cobblestones. A fang pierced my lower lip as I hit the ground.

I lay there stunned, my mouth filling with blood. I got up quickly and looked through the gaping opening into the pub catching sight of Flame still being held by two soldiers.

I spoke the words to myself, hoping she would hear them the same way I heard her voice in my head.

I will come back for you.

And then, as soldiers began to rush toward me, I sprang down the snowy lane and disappeared into the thick forests of the Dunfeld countryside.

ON SALE NOW

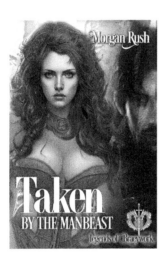

I hope you enjoyed this preview of the next book in the Legends of Braeyork series.

Taken by the Manbeast,

Book 2 of the Legends of Braeyork

by Morgan Rush

On sale now at Amazon (Kindle).

Print version available soon!